LITTLE LEAGUE
GIANT

LITTLE LEAGUE GIANT

by DON CREIGHTON

STECK-VAUGHN
COMPANY

AUSTIN, TEXAS

Library of Congress Catalog Card Number 65-12084
Copyright © 1965 by Steck-Vaughn Company, Austin, Texas
All rights reserved.
Printed and bound in the United States of America

Bonanza for the Bears

AT THE EDGE of the Millbrook High School athletic field was a card table bearing a large, hand-lettered sign that read MILLBROOK LITTLE LEAGUE. TRYOUTS 1—4 P. M. REGISTRATION FEE—$1.00.

Behind the table, in a folding chair, sat a brawny-looking man in a blue baseball cap and a red T-shirt with MILLBROOK LITTLE LEAGUE spelled out across it in white letters.

A little farther away, a thin man in the same kind of T-shirt and a green cap was pinning a sheet of paper bearing a large number 86 onto the back of a very small boy. Still farther away was a group of boys already numbered. Watching them was a group of men carrying clipboards and wearing caps of orange, black, purple, or red.

Chris Sorensen moved close to the table and held out a little bundle of papers. They were damp from being held in his hand so long, for Chris was the last in what had been a long line. Now he couldn't delay any longer, for he was the only one left.

"Sorry, sir," the man in the blue cap said, "your son will have to—" Then, looking up, he hastily corrected himself. "I mean—your little brother will have to hand in his own application."

Chris felt his face grow hot. He shuffled his feet in the dust, swallowed hard, and finally muttered, "It's me, sir."

"*You?*" The man's bushy eyebrows shot up. His sharp gray eyes, in a pointed face that reminded Chris of a gnome's in a storybook, glared in disbelief.

At last the man took the papers. He unfolded them and put the crisp dollar bill to one side. Then he examined the application blank Chris had carefully filled out the night before.

"Your name Christian Sorensen?"

"Yes, sir."

"Hm. Never seen you around before."

"No, sir. We moved here—three weeks ago, just about. From Dover Falls," Chris said.

"Hm. Seems like I ought to know that name— Christian Sorensen. Can't think where from, but it rings a bell." The man rubbed his chin thoughtfully.

Chris said nothing. After a moment the man gave him another sharp look. "You'll be thirteen—when?"

"October the second, sir," Chris said. He added rather pleadingly, "My birth certificate's right there, sir. You can look."

The man examined the paper, seeming to ponder every word, before he handed it back. "Seems to be in order," he admitted.

Chris let out a long breath of relief. That part was over, anyway. Maybe it would turn out to be the worst part. If only he were back in Dover Falls!

But he knew it was no use wishing that again, any more than it had been the thousands of times he'd wished it before in the past three weeks. Though his knees still felt wobbly, he made himself move toward the others who were trying out for the Millbrook Little League.

Some older boys were dividing the candidates into four groups, sending each to a different part of the field. They stared hard at Chris for a moment, then ignored him. But he tagged stubbornly along.

"You kids will try out for hitting first," their guide announced. "You swing three times, then bunt twice. Remember that, now! When you're through, go to the other side for the running. Understand?"

There was a chorus of "Okay, Bob!" and "We got it!"

The stocky, dark-haired Bob stared at Chris again. "You sure you belong here, kid?" he asked. Chris nodded, his face burning again.

An extremely small, freckle-faced boy put on a helmet and picked up a bat. Bob tossed the first pitch gently over the plate. The little boy swung and sent a sharp drive past the pitcher. One of the watching men wrote something on a paper in his clipboard.

If only he were back in Dover Falls—Chris had promised his father he'd try not to wish that any more. But he couldn't help it.

Back in Dover Falls nobody would have asked to see his birth certificate, or stared at him in disbelief, or asked him if he was sure he belonged here. Back in Dover Falls everybody was used to Chris Sorensen's being five-feet-eleven and weighing a hundred and forty-five. As far as they were concerned, that was the way Chris was meant to be. His size belonged to him, like his bright blue eyes, his fair curly hair, and his large, gleaming-white teeth.

And, back in Dover Falls, nobody stuck a number on your back and made you parade around like a steer at an auction. No strange, sharp-eyed men watched every move you made and wrote it down. The Dover Falls Little League had tryouts, of course. But they were casual, friendly events, more sociable than competitive. Dover Falls was such a small town that by using every boy of proper age, it could just manage to fill out its four-team league. In Dover Falls every manager knew every boy and just about what he could do. By tryout day it was pretty well settled who would be on each team, so nobody had anything to worry about.

While Chris had been daydreaming of Dover Falls, the line had been moving briskly along. He realized with a start that it was his turn to bat. He fumbled with the three helmets that had been provided. As he might have known, they were all too small. He jammed the largest one on his head, so tight it pinched his ears and made his head ache. He picked up a bat and walked to the plate.

Bob looked Chris slowly up and down. Then he shrugged his shoulders, and threw. The ball came slowly right across the plate. Chris swung.

Someone yelled, "Wow!" Someone else gave a long whistle. The ball was still going—beyond the edge of the field and into a flower bed near the schoolhouse.

As a boy ran to recover it, one of the managers called, "That's enough! Can't afford to lose any baseballs. Go on over to the running line."

Chris thought he did all right at running. How could he help it, when his legs were so much longer than anybody else's? But he missed all but one of the fly balls hit to him and every one of the grounders and bouncers. When it was over and he trudged in, the last to have the number taken off his back, he wished he'd never come to the tryout.

"That's all," the man in the green cap said, as he undid the pin on Chris's back. His voice sounded like one of those recorded announcements on the telephone, from saying it so often. "We'll let you know in a day or two."

Head down and shoulders drooping, Chris dragged his feet across the grass toward home. His course took him close to where the managers, in their different-colored caps, were gathered in a tight cluster.

Chris didn't mean to listen to what they were saying, but the first words that reached him were so interesting he slowed down, straining his ears to hear all he could.

"—anything like that Sorensen kid," one of them said excitedly. "What a clout!"

"Some people are born lucky," another voice complained.

There was a chortling laugh. Chris glanced quickly toward the voices—just long enough to see that the laugh had come from the man in the blue cap. Sitting behind the table, he'd looked of average height. But now Chris could see that he was by far the shortest of the group, and that made him look more than ever like a shrewd, kindly gnome. His rather high-pitched voice sounded exactly right for a gnome, too.

"I'll let you boys fight for the rest, but we've got first place right here!" crowed the man in the blue cap. There was the slap of an open hand against the paper in his clipboard, and another satisfied chuckle. "Yes, sir! Struck it rich this time. A real bonanza for the Bears."

CHAPTER 2

Maybe a White Elephant

"WELL, I GUESS you're not a pitcher." Mr. Snedecker, manager of the Bears, took off the catcher's gear and settled his blue cap back on his head.

Chris walked slowly in from the mound. "I'm not, sir?" he asked mournfully.

The top of Mr. Snedecker's head reached hardly higher than the middle of Chris's chest, and he had to bend his neck 'way back to look Chris in the eye. Because that seemed so uncomfortable, Chris stepped back a couple of paces to make it easier. Mr. Snedecker put his hands on his hips and shook his head emphatically.

"My goodness, boy! You don't throw that ball hard enough to break a pane of glass," he declared.

"Mr. Goodman, that was my manager back in Dover Falls, said my control was good," Chris said.

"Sure it is! Comes over the plate every time in the same spot, nice and easy. Why, my goodness, boy! The hitters would clobber it."

Chris nodded, biting his lip. He could feel the hot redness flooding his face, as it always did when he was upset or ashamed. Mr. Snedecker was right. That was exactly what had happened, in the game he'd pitched back in Dover Falls.

"Well, now!" Mr. Snedecker smiled broadly, and rubbed his hands briskly together. "Just because you're not a pitcher, you don't have to feel bad. Pitchers are born, boy. You can teach 'em. You can improve 'em. But you can't make 'em. Now, on that application form you said you'd played every position for your team in Dover Falls. That right?"

"Yes, sir," Chris said. He was feeling pretty good again. Mr. Snedecker's disappointment in finding that Chris didn't pitch as well as he'd expected hadn't been such a shock as it might have been, after what his father had told him last night.

Chris had walked home from the tryouts feeling on top of the world. All the way, he'd kept thinking about what the man in the blue cap had called him—a bonanza! He'd heard the word many times before and knew it meant something good, though he wasn't sure exactly what.

As soon as he got home he looked it up. "A rich vein of ore. Hence, a source of great profit."

Chris grinned happily at the idea of somebody's thinking he was so valuable. Maybe it wouldn't be so bad in Millbrook, after all. Nobody in Dover Falls had ever called him a bonanza.

At the dinner table, Chris couldn't wait to tell the family about the tryouts, and about what he'd heard afterward. His sisters were too young to know what it all meant—Hilda was four and Tina was only two—but they recognized the happiness in his voice and squealed with admiration and delight.

His mother had said, "Why Chris! I think that's wonderful!"

His father had nodded without saying anything. But later, when Chris's mother had gone to put his sisters to bed, Chris had known his father was getting ready to say something. He could always tell, when his father took extra care in lighting his pipe and then puffed at it methodically, that he was arranging in his mind something he wanted to say.

Chris had waited uneasily. It was impossible to tell whether his father was about to scold him for something bad he'd done or commend him for something good. Or whether maybe he was only preparing to ask a question or give a bit of advice.

"Pretty nice, being called some sort of treasure," Chris's father had remarked at last.

Chris had grinned, with relief and pride. "It sure is!"

"Only thing—" Chris's father had paused, taking another leisurely puff at his pipe. "Be better if it was the end of the season he said it."

Chris had nodded reluctant agreement. Now that his father had said it, he knew that thought had been lurking in the back of his mind and he'd been trying not to admit it was there.

"Big fellows like us—sometimes people forget we're just ordinary fellows. So we can't ever forget it, ourselves. See what I mean, Chris?"

"I—I guess so." Chris knew he was lucky to have a father six-foot-seven, who knew what it was like when most people had to look up at you. He knew his father had been right to remind him they didn't always see you the way you really were. But—last night he'd almost wished he could have had a little longer to gloat over the thought of being a treasure.

Still, it was true people did expect too much of you when you were big. Chris had learned that early in life.

"Aren't you ashamed to cry—a big boy like you?"

someone said, when he fell and skinned his knee. That was long before he started to school.

"You mean a big boy like you can't tie his shoe-laces?" That was in kindergarten. Plenty of others couldn't tie their shoelaces either. But they weren't so big.

And,"Why don't you pick on somebody your own size?" That was in fourth grade. And the boy who'd started the fight had been a sixth-grader, twice as strong as Chris and three times as well coordinated. But not as big.

Chris looked longingly at the other Bears. They were spread across the outfield, taking turns chasing the flies Bob was hitting to them. This was the same stocky, dark-haired boy who'd pitched at the tryouts, and he'd be helping Mr. Snedecker manage the Bears during the season. Chris would have given anything to be over there with the rest. If only nobody were expecting anything special of him—

"My goodness, boy! Will you stop daydreaming and listen?" Mr. Snedecker demanded.

Chris returned to reality with a jolt. "I'm sorry, sir."

"I *said*, how in the world could you play every

position in the lineup when you're left-handed? Tell me that!"

Chris scuffed his feet uneasily, then stopped when he saw what a cloud of dust he was raising. "I don't know, sir. I just did. That is, we all did, sir."

"You played *shortstop* left-handed? And *second* base? And *third?*"

"Yes, sir," Chris admitted. "You see, our manager thought it was more fun that way. So everybody'd have a chance to see which he liked best."

For a moment Chris was afraid Mr. Snedecker was going to cry. Then he thought he must be going to laugh. But he did neither. He simply turned his back and walked away, stood motionless for a moment, then turned and walked back.

"Now, then," Mr. Snedecker said in a soft, deliberately calm voice, "maybe you're a catcher. It's possible to be a good left-handed catcher. Not likely, but possible. Let's give it a try. We haven't got a mitt for a left-hander, so just use your regular glove. I won't throw hard."

"Yes, sir," Chris said agreeably.

A few minutes later Mr. Snedecker came off the mound, his shoulders drooping. "You're not a catcher, either," he groaned. "Too bad, because you can reach that ball no matter where it's pitched, and you can hang onto it. It's your arm again. You can't make that throw down to second."

"No, sir," Chris said mournfully.

"Can't understand it," Mr. Snedecker said, frowning. "A big boy like you, having such a weak arm. Could be just that you never learned to use it right. If that's it, I can teach you. But it'll take time. There's got to be something you can do right now. Anybody who can hit a ball like that one at the tryouts has got to be in our lineup. You get over there with the outfielders, and we'll start putting our team together."

"Yes, sir!" Chris trotted away, but not quickly enough.

Echoing in his ears as he joined the other boys, the tallest of whom was barely shoulder-high on him, was Mr. Snedecker's lament. "Oh, brother! Instead of a bonanza, maybe we've got a white elephant."

CHAPTER 3

Like Father, Like Son

"CHRIS WILL BE our right fielder, Mr. Sorensen," said Mr. Snedecker, smiling.

The final practice was over. All the boys, the fathers, and the managers of other teams who had come to watch were gone. Besides Mr. Snedecker and Bob, only Chris and his father remained. Bob was out in left field, working with rake and shovel to level out some small bumps and hollows.

Chris glanced up at his father. As usual, his face was placid and expressionless. He nodded, took a meditative puff at his pipe, and blinked his mild, sky-blue eyes. Impossible to tell whether he was happy that Chris had won a place in the starting lineup or whether he was disappointed in what that place had turned out to be.

Right field! That was where a manager put his worst player. "Anyway, he can't hurt us out there," he'd heard more than once back in Dover Falls of some kid who wasn't good for much of anything.

That must have been what Mr. Snedecker had said to Bob as they had conferred over the Bears' lineup. Right field was the only place to put a white elephant, as long as a manager had let himself be stuck with one.

Chris was thankful he hadn't mentioned anything at home about being called a white elephant. That was another of those expressions, like "bonanza," that he'd heard many times without ever stopping to wonder exactly what it meant. But he'd been pretty sure it wasn't a compliment, and again he'd gone to the dictionary.

"Anything which seems to be desirable but turns out to be troublesome." That was what the definition boiled down to, after a great many words about oriental potentates and their expensive beasts.

So, ever since the Bears' first practice, Chris had known that Mr. Snedecker believed he was more trouble than he was worth. At nearly every practice since, Mr. Snedecker had called aside one or two boys and talked to them privately for a few moments. Those boys were being cut, sent down to the minors because they weren't good enough for Mr. Snedecker's Bears. Each time, Chris had expected to hear his own name called. But it hadn't been. Now that only fifteen boys remained, he was still one of them. And, from what Mr. Snedecker had said to his father, it seemed that he was actually to be one of the nine who'd be in the starting line-up for tomorrow's game. But he couldn't imagine why.

"Glad I had a chance to watch your practice this evening," Chris's father said. "Makes me proud Chris managed to qualify for a team here in Mill-brook. I'd never realized young boys could play such good baseball. In Dover Falls, where we come from, Little League is a pretty casual affair. Oh, we stick by the rules as best we can. But in a town as small as Dover Falls, material's pretty thin. Playing talent, *and* managing talent. Practices are sloppy by your standards. Lots of fooling around. But—this surprised me, Mr. Snedecker—I believe your Millbrook boys enjoy these tough practices more than the Dover Falls kids do our easy ones."

"Of course they do! Any kid likes a tough job better than an easy one. Ever hear of a boy getting all fired up about walking a few blocks to school? But mention a fifty-mile hike and he'll be rarin' to go. We aim high, here in Millbrook. Any boy who makes one of our teams has something to be proud of. Even the ones who don't quite make it can feel they've been tested in tough competition. They learn a lot, too."

Chris's father nodded. "Yes, I expect one of Millbrook's minor league teams could whip the Dover Falls champs with no trouble at all. The difference is amazing."

"Well—" Mr. Snedecker craned his neck to look up at Mr. Sorensen. "If you'll pardon my saying so, it shows in your boy. He's missed out on some fundamentals, and he's formed some bad habits. If only you'd moved here a few years ago—but you didn't, so there's no use complaining. Do you think you'd have time to work with Chris at home, maybe an hour each day?"

"Sorry, Mr. Snedecker," Chris's father said. "Fact is, I never played baseball myself. I expect I'd do more harm than good."

"But—" Chris saw that Mr. Snedecker was staring at his father intently, his face twisted in a baffled frown. "Sorensen. Christian Sorensen. That name meant something to me, first time I heard it. And now your face. I've seen your picture in the newspaper. I've seen it on the sports page. Not lately, maybe. But I know I've seen it many a time."

"It's been nice meeting you, Mr. Snedecker. Ready, Chris?" Mr. Sorensen threw over his shoulder as he started to move away.

"Wait! I remember now!" Mr. Snedecker's voice was shrill with triumph. He was grinning broadly as he hurried to catch up with them. "Sure! You're the Big Swede. You played fullback for State, back when nobody in the country could beat 'em. You made everybody's All-American. How could I forget?"

Mr. Sorensen's face had reddened, but its calm expression was unchanged. He shrugged his massive shoulders. "That was over twenty years ago. Everybody ought to forget it."

"Forget it? I should say not! Hey, Bob! Come here. There's somebody you've got to meet."

Chris waited uneasily while Bob shook his father's hand. "Sorensen? The Big Swede?" Bob seemed as astonished and as impressed as if he had been meeting the President of the United States. "Yes, sir, I've heard about you. How you never looked like so much in practice or when things were going right. But then, when your team got in a tight spot—look out! People still talk about the way you'd charge through the opposition. Like a bulldozer through brush, I remember somebody saying. Sure wish I'd been around to see you play."

"You're right, Bob. You really missed something," Mr. Snedecker agreed. "Still—you know, sir, your Chris must be mighty like what you were at his age. Like father, like son—or so they say."

Chris couldn't help wondering, as this talk went on, whether Mr. Snedecker had been just pretending. Maybe he'd known all along who his father was. Sure—he must have! That would explain why he'd kept him on the Bears, why he'd given him a place in the starting lineup. Mr. Snedecker admired his father so much, he'd have kept him on the team even if he'd never seen a baseball before. Probably he'd taken him because he expected him to play baseball the way his father had played football. And then, when it turned out he couldn't he'd kept him just for the glory of having the Big Swede's son on his team.

"You know," Mr. Snedecker went on excitedly, "we've been trying for years to get a kids' football league started in Millbrook. Now I'll bet we can do it! Would you consider heading it up, just at first? Wait—don't make up your mind now. Think about it. It'd be a great thing for the kids. But it's a job to organize, raise funds, and get managers and officials. Suppose you don't have much time to give? If we can say you're behind us—the Big Swede, greatest player ever to come out of this part of the country—that's all we'll need."

Chris's father became very busy, packing fresh tobacco into his pipe and lighting it. At last he said, "I'll think about it. But I'll tell you this right now. If you spread it around about Chris being the Big Swede's son, you can forget it. He's entitled to live with his own name and make his own record—at least for this baseball season."

Mr. Snedecker's face fell, but after a moment he forced a smile. "Sure, sure!" he agreed. "We won't say a word. Remember that, Bob. Not a word! But don't blame us if the news gets around. Other people are sure to recognize you, too."

"You'd be surprised how many people don't," Chris's father said solemnly, as he turned away.

CHAPTER 4

A Mysterious Sickness

Now CHRIS KNEW why a smart manager like Mr. Snedecker had let himself be stuck with a white elephant. It was because the white elephant's father was the man who could put over a kid football league in Millbrook. And how could you expect a man to do you a favor if you cut his son off your team? That must have been the way Mr. Snedecker figured. So, to keep the Big Swede happy, Chris had been kept on the Bears. And he would be kept, and he would play, no matter how much of a white elephant he turned out to be. He'd be in right field, where he couldn't do much damage. But he'd play.

The whole thing seemed so obvious that Chris was surprised to realize his father had no idea what was going on. "Tomorrow's the big day, then?" Mr. Sorensen asked as they drove toward home. "You'll want to get to bed early tonight. Be ready to march in the parade and then play your first game."

Chris shook his head. "We don't play tomorrow. Only four teams can play in the doubleheader. Our first game's Wednesday at six, against the Colts. And Mr. Snedecker told me I don't have to march in the parade."

"Don't *have* to march in the parade?" Chris's mother demanded, when he repeated the information to her. "Why do you say *have to?* I should think you'd be thrilled to be part of a big parade with *two* bands. They tell me that Little League opening day in Millbrook is almost as important as the Fourth of July!"

Chris scowled down at the toes of his dusty sneakers. "It's because my shoes and pants haven't come yet. How do you think I'd feel, marching in sneaks and blue jeans, and everybody else in uniform?"

"Oh—I'd forgotten. Yes, I understand, Chris. It was nice of Mr. Snedecker to excuse you. I'm sure the things will be here in time for the game Wednesday."

Chris knew his mother tried hard to understand how he felt, but he knew she never could. She herself was just the right size. She'd never had to hear a man say, in a voice loud enough to reach everyone in the Sport Shop, "I'm sorry, we haven't anything that large."

His words had taken Chris by surprise. In Dover Falls nobody had bothered with special shoes, but had just played in sneakers. Chris had had no idea he'd have trouble getting the Little League shoes Mr. Snedecker had told him he'd need.

Chris's face burned again, remembering how the man had continued in that same loud voice, "We've never had a call for size twelve. But we can get a pair from the manufacturer in a few days."

The day after that, the Bears went to Mr. Snedecker's house for their uniforms. First Mr. Snedecker gave each boy a blue cap like his own. The large size fitted Chris perfectly. Then he opened the big carton in which the Bears' uniforms had been stored for the winter.

In Dover Falls they'd never had real uniforms—only T-shirts, with the team name across the front. Chris couldn't wait to put on the gray flannel with bright blue letters.

Mr. Snedecker lined everybody up according to size, beginning with little Tommy O'Brien the second baseman and ending with Chris.

"Makes things easy, the way they arrange these uniforms," he said cheerfully. "Number one's the smallest, and right up they go to number fifteen for the biggest. We've never had a boy yet big enough to fill that one up. So here you are, Chris. Give it a try."

Chris put on the shirt. Ignoring the fact that it was a little short, he said, "Just fine, Mr. Snedecker."

Then he pulled on the pants. The waist was a little too large, and there was plenty of room in the seat. It was plain that someone had anticipated having a fat boy on a team. But nobody had foreseen a boy as tall as Chris. He couldn't even stretch the legs down over his knees.

There was a burst of laughter from the other boys, at the sight of Chris's bony knees and long legs emerging from the too-short pants. Mr. Snedecker hushed them quickly, but Chris saw that he'd had to try hard to keep from laughing himself.

"My goodness, boy!" he cried. "I never thought you could do it. But don't worry. We'll get you a pair right away. Lucky it's not the shirt, with the letters and all. Just a plain pair of gray pants."

Watching Saturday's parade with his parents was fun. Not marching gave him a chance to look over the teams. Right behind the school band came the Tigers, last year's champs. They wore cream-colored uniforms trimmed in orange. Then the Stags, in white with black trim. Then the Bears, light gray and blue.

Even after practicing with the Bears, Chris could remember the names of only a few boys. He recognized the two red-headed brothers, Kenneth and Tommy O'Brien, and a boy they called Howie. He was skinny and wore glasses. The rest looked so much alike in their uniforms, and so different from their usual selves, that he couldn't tell them apart.

After the Bears came the Wildcats, in gray and red. Then the Lions, in white and green. Last the Colts, in gray trimmed with purple.

The Little League teams were followed by the teams of the minor league, those of the girls' softball league, and a crowd of small boys from the beginners' clinic. Cars filled with officials followed, and last the Fire Department band, blaring away with "Take Me Out to the Ball Game." Chris and his parents joined the crowd in applauding for them all, but they saved their cheers for their favorite team, the Bears.

Afterward, Chris's mother took the little girls home, and Chris and his father watched the games. They saw the Stags trail by a run for five innings, then stage a rally to beat the Lions three to one in an errorless game. Then, in the second contest, the

Tiger pitcher gave up only one hit as his team scored a three-to-nothing victory over the Wildcats.

"Well!" Mr. Sorensen said as they turned toward home. "They play a different brand of baseball here from what we've been used to at Dover Falls. Back there, they think they're doing well if the walks and the errors don't outnumber the hits and the runs. Guess I kind of took it for granted Mr. Snedecker and his Bears were something special, but it seems they're only what's expected in Millbrook. A boy can be proud to wear any one of those uniforms. And, Wednesday you'll be wearing one."

Chris nodded, and tried to smile. His father thought he'd be wearing that uniform because he deserved to. How long could he go on believing that?

    ♢   ♢   ♢   ♢   ♢

Wednesday came, and the pants and shoes hadn't arrived. Mr. Snedecker had told Chris it would be all right to wear the sneakers and blue jeans he wore for practice, along with the blue cap and the uniform shirt. Nobody would think a thing about it, Mr. Snedecker had assured him.

But Chris knew better. He made one last, desperate call to the Sport Shop, but the news was the same. Nothing had arrived.

Sneakers in hand, Chris went into the kitchen where his mother was giving his sisters their supper, and dropped heavily into a chair. Slowly he bent over to slip on one sneaker and tie it.

"Oooh!" he groaned, as he straightened up again.

His mother turned quickly. "What's the matter?"

"I don't feel so good," he mumbled.

His mother looked surprised. "You certainly look healthy enough. And you've seemed fine all day. You even cut the grass after you came from school. What's the trouble—your throat again?"

Chris shook his head. "It's—uh—my head. And my stomach feels funny."

Chris's mother put her cheek against his forehead for a moment. "No fever. What in the world could it be?" She sighed, and shook her head. "Better get to bed. If you're not all right in the morning, I'll call a doctor."

In his room, Chris stretched out on his bed. Groaning softly, he tried to convince himself there really was an ache in his head and a funny feeling in his stomach. It was not as easy as convincing his mother had been.

There was the sound of a car in the driveway.

Then the back door opened and closed. Chris heard his father's voice greeting his mother and sisters. Then he heard, "Where's Chris? Isn't he ready to go?"

His mother's answer was too soft for Chris to make out the words. So was his father's voice when he spoke again. Then his father's footsteps came across the hall and mounted the stairs. Chris lay still, his eyes closed. He could feel his father standing in the doorway, watching him. Chris hoped he'd think he was asleep and go away.

But he didn't, and at last Chris opened his eyes.

"Mama tells me you're sick," his father said. Chris nodded. "Your head, she says. Does it ache much, Chris?"

Miserably, Chris muttered, "No, sir."

His father nodded solemnly. "I think I know what ails you. It's in your head, but it's not an ache. And that trouble in your head brings on the funny feeling in your stomach. I've had that sickness myself. There's no medicine that will help it."

Chris's heart gave a little jump of alarm. What was this mysterious complaint, that he hadn't even known existed?

"Mama said you must feel very bad, even though you looked well and had no fever," Chris's father went on slowly. "Otherwise, you'd never miss your first Little League game in Millbrook."

"That's right," Chris muttered.

"But you're not going to miss that game," his father told him solemnly. "You're going to cure yourself. You're going to walk out on that field, and by the time the game starts you'll be feeling fine."

"But—I haven't got my uniform pants. Or the right kind of shoes."

"Now, Chris! You know it's not really the pants or the shoes. Is it?"

"Why not?" Chris demanded indignantly. "How'd you like to go to work in sneaks and blue jeans?" But, as his father kept looking at him calmly and saying nothing, he gave in. "Oh, all right! I wouldn't care, only everybody'll know *why*. They'll laugh. And they'll say things like, 'How can he really be only twelve?' You know!"

"Yes, I know." Mr. Sorensen laid a big hand gently on Chris's shoulder. "That's part of being a big fellow—extra big. Son, you're big because God made you that way. You can't change it. You can't hide it. You can't run away from it. It goes with being yourself—like being a boy instead of a girl. Being ashamed of what you are, when you can't change it, is a sickness. The only cure is just to go ahead being yourself, doing what you're supposed to do."

"Guess you're right, Dad," Chris said. Slowly, he sat up and began to lace on his sneakers.

[CHAPTER 5]

So Far, So Good

WHAT CHRIS'S FATHER had told him turned out to be only partly true. When the Bears took the field, he didn't feel sick, but neither did he feel fine.

What he'd feared most, the stares and laughter of the crowd, had turned out to be not so bad as he'd expected. In the first place, the crowd was much smaller than the one on opening day. In the second place, the looks and the few audible remarks had been mostly friendly and admiring. In the third place, trying to remember everything Mr. Snedecker and Bob had told him had kept him too busy to worry about the people watching.

What kept Chris from feeling really fine, as he trotted out to right field, was that his head felt stuffed to bursting with instructions.

Back in Dover Falls, playing the outfield had seemed simple. You were assigned a section of the grass between the base lines and the fence. If a ball came into your territory, you got hold of it the best way you could and sent it back to the infield.

But here in Millbrook it wasn't that simple. "Call for those fly balls!" "Remember how many are out!" "Never take your eye off the batter!" "Watch those base runners—know where you'll throw the ball if you get it!" "Check the wind—a look at the flag will tell you how it's blowing!" "Back up those infielders!" "Watch for my signals—didn't you see me wave you back?" "Remember to allow for a high bounce on hard ground."

All these words echoed through Chris's head as he watched the first Colt batter approach the plate. So many things to think about all at the same time. And he was sure there were dozens more—probably the most important ones—that had escaped him completely.

Chris stood leaning a little forward, heels off the ground, knees bent, in the position Mr. Snedecker said made sure he'd be ready to move fast in any direction. But instead he felt as heavy and stiff as a statue and just about as ready to move.

The batter took two balls, a strike, then two more balls. As he trotted to first, Chris glanced around at the other Bears. They seemed cool and relaxed.

Freckle-faced Mark Ramsey, the shortstop, called cheerfully, "Okay, you guys! Let's get two."

Over at third, Sandy Baker edged a little farther from the bag, but his mind seemed entirely occupied with blowing an enormous bubble of gum.

Even pitcher Kenneth O'Brien, whom nobody ever called anything but Kayo, seemed untroubled by having walked his first batter of the season.

But, Chris thought, these others had had years to get used to the Millbrook way of playing ball. They'd been able to learn a little at a time, instead of having everything thrown at them at once.

Now another Colt batter was at the plate. He swung and missed. The next pitch was very low, and as Jerry Jones—the Bears' catcher—scooped it out of the dust, the runner sped for second. But he had underestimated Jerry. His throw went hard and straight to second, where Tommy made the tag with no trouble. The batter struck out, and the next popped up to short to end the inning.

Chris let out a long breath of relief. One inning

gone, and he hadn't needed to move. Why, sure!
This was right field, where hardly anything ever
happened, and even a poor player couldn't do much
harm.

As the Bears prepared to bat, Mr. Snedecker spoke
to Chris almost apologetically. "Hope you don't
feel bad that I've got you batting eighth. Didn't
want you under pressure right at the start, you see.
You'll soon be moving up where you belong."

"Oh, I don't mind, sir," Chris said. He was only
surprised he wasn't at the very end of the order. In
practice after practice, he'd never managed to get
good wood on the ball. The Bears ought to be
hoping he'd never get up at all.

A few minutes later it looked as if he might bat
in the very first inning. The Colt shortstop fumbled
Sandy's grounder. Then Jerry smashed a line drive
down the third base line that seemed a sure hit. But
the Colt third baseman made a diving catch, then
threw to first to double off the surprised Sandy.
Mark Ramsey drew a walk to re-awaken the Bears'
hopes, but was forced when the Colt second baseman scooped up Kayo's grounder and stepped on
the bag.

Once more in the second inning, right field was as
peaceful as a ghost town. True, the Colts scored a

run and took the lead. But there was nothing Chris could have done to stop that, as the Colts' first baseman drew a walk, stole second, went to third on a wild pitch, and came home on a sacrifice bunt.

When Tommy O'Brien led off the bottom of the second with a single, Chris knew nothing but a double play could save him from batting this time. And he surely wouldn't wish for that. He pulled on the largest helmet, and tried to loosen up by swinging a couple of bats.

Now his head was full of things he'd been told about hitting. "Stand easy—up on your toes!" "Time your stride!" "Watch that ball all the way!" "Keep your swing level!" "Follow through!" There was little enough time to think in the field, but at the plate the ball was past you before you could begin to collect your thoughts.

Tommy, not half Chris's size, didn't seem to need time to think. After taking a called strike and a ball too high, he whipped his bat around and drove a sharp single between short and third.

Next up was another small boy, the left fielder. Chris couldn't remember his name until, as the count reached three and two, Sandy burst into shrill song. The tune was a familiar one, but the words had been somewhat altered.

Darling, I am growing older,
Sitting on this bench all day.
Take that bat off of your shoulder
Before my hair starts turning gray.

Laughter swept along the benches and rippled through the bleachers. Somebody called, "Come on, Darling! Hit one—just for me?"

Of course! Chris wondered how he could have forgotten. The kid's name was Bill Darling. Having a name like that must be awful—almost as bad as being five-feet-eleven inches tall.

But Bill Darling gave no sign that he had heard. His round face blandly cheerful, he hit the next pitch and sent a long fly straight over second base and nearly to the fence. Though the center fielder made the catch, Tommy was able to tag up and go to second.

Pat DeCarlo, the Bears' center fielder, missed a mighty swing for a third strike, and that meant it was time for Chris to see what he could do.

As he walked to the plate, Chris felt as if he were growing bigger, heavier, more awkward, with each step. Every muscle and joint felt set and rigid, like hardened cement. His fingers were stiff and tight around the bat handle so that he felt he couldn't let go if he wanted to. His teeth were clenched so hard his jaws and throat ached.

The Colt pitcher stood rubbing the ball between his hands. He was under five feet and slight of build. Chris thought he must appear to the spectators like a brave little David facing a brutal Goliath.

Excited voices from his teammates called encouragement. "You can do it, Chris!" "Let's see one right over the fence." "Yeah! Like the one you hit in the tryouts, kid."

The seconds dragged on, an endless misery. At last the Colt catcher called time out, and trotted to the mound. Heads together, he and his pitcher conferred. When the catcher returned, he crouched far to the right of the plate, while the pitcher lobbed the ball into his mitt.

There was a chorus of groans from the Bears' bench and sighs of relief from the Colts. But Chris felt only a great thankfulness, like a condemned man who has won a last-minute reprieve. It was a good thing the Colt pitcher hadn't known he was so paralyzed with fear that he'd never have been able to move the bat, no matter how fat a pitch had come across the plate. A strikeout by Howie ended the inning.

But the knowledge that he wouldn't have to bat

again for quite a while let Chris relax just a little. And when Mark led off the fourth with a single and Kayo followed with a home run that put the Bears in the lead, he relaxed a little more.

Right field continued as free from activity as if it had been in the next county. Chris's next trip to the plate was as lead-off man in the fifth, which meant that not so much depended on what he did. This time he felt that if he really had to he might be able to lift the bat from his shoulder. But the Colts' pitcher was so careful not to give him anything good that he drew another walk.

At last came the top of the sixth. It was the Colts' last chance to catch up. Chris took his place in right field. Only three more outs and the game would be over.

So far Kayo had pitched a great game. He'd given up only one hit in five innings. But the first Colt batter, a stocky kid with glasses who'd gone in at third base only last inning, popped a very harmless-looking fly that dropped in front of the center fielder for a single. The catcher followed with a drive to left for another. A strikeout followed. Then, after a long-drawn struggle in which he fouled off eight pitches, the Colts' second baseman drew a walk.

Bases loaded. Only one out. Chris tensed with dread as he realized that if the Colts scored, he'd be third up in the bottom of the sixth. No matter how scared the Colts' pitcher might be, he'd hardly give anything away at that stage of a close game. Then he'd discover how foolish he'd been to be scared at all.

The Colts' right fielder struck out. Just one more. . . .

The batter was a very fat boy who came straight off the bench. Chris glanced at Mr. Snedecker. He was motioning the fielders back, and he didn't stop until they were nearly at the fence.

The fat boy stood with bat poised, a confident smile on his round face. As Kayo's first pitch whizzed toward him he took a mighty swing. There was a solid crack as bat met ball.

It was lined straight and hard toward right field, just high enough to clear the fence. The crowd was on its feet, screaming with excitement. The runners were on their way.

Chris's feet seemed made of lead, and his legs of iron. He couldn't have taken a step if his life had depended on it. But he could stretch—lift on his toes, reach high with his long, bony right arm. The ball thudded into his glove so hard that the shock tingled all the way to his elbow.

For a moment there was dead silence. Then cheers and applause even louder than before. As Chris trotted in, still holding the ball, the Bears swarmed around him.

"What a catch! What a *catch!*"

"Won the game for us, that's all."

"*Boy*, what a catch!"

Chris couldn't speak, even to thank the fellows for the nice things they were saying. His face seemed on fire, and inside, too, he was burning with shame. How could they say he'd won the game, when all he'd done was to stand where Mr. Snedecker had put him and hold up his glove? Had they forgotten that Kayo had done some tremendous pitching, and hit a home run besides?

But even Kayo was joining in. He gripped Chris's arm, a big grin on his usually solemn face. "You sure saved that one for me, Chris! What a catch!"

So far, so good, Chris thought when the Bears had been dismissed and he headed for his father's car. So far, so good. But how long could a guy go on being so lucky?

CHAPTER 6

No Refuge in Right Field

"YOU DID ALL RIGHT, CHRIS," his father told him.
"Wonderful!" his mother cried when she heard
about the game. "You've made a good start."

At school, on the playground, everywhere Chris
went, somebody mentioned the game. Some con-
gratulated him on robbing the Colt pinch-hitter of
his home run. Others admired the way he'd scared
the Colts' pitcher into putting him on twice in a row.

At first Chris tried to protest. He'd just been
lucky. But nobody paid any attention, so he gave
up and smiled his thanks. He even began to wonder
if maybe he hadn't been pretty good. Everybody
else thought so.

Chris began to look forward hopefully to Saturday's game with the Lions. He needn't worry this time about looking different, for the new shoes and pants had arrived. Besides, he'd survived the ordeal of facing a Millbrook crowd. And he'd had a chance to get acquainted with his teammates, since they'd been through a real game together. If he really was a better player than he'd thought, this game would give him a chance to prove it.

As the Bears took the field to warm up, Chris felt surefooted in the Little League shoes with their earth-gripping rubber cleats. The new pants were more loosely cut than his jeans and gave him more freedom to move. Today everything would be different.

Chris handled the fly balls Bob hit to him in practice with no trouble. Then, batting, he put the first two pitches over the fence. Beaming, Mr. Snedecker waved him out of the box.

The other Bears pounded Chris on the back as he walked away. Over by the other dugout, the Lions were staring open-mouthed at the treetops where the two balls he'd hit had disappeared.

Today the Lions were the home team, the Bears first at bat. Chris had been moved up a notch so that this time he was batting seventh instead of eighth. That seemed like a good sign. He almost hoped that this time he'd get to the plate in the first inning.

But he didn't come close. Tommy O'Brien, leading off, was out on a grounder that the second baseman scooped up easily and flipped to first. Bill Darling put one in the same spot, and was out just as easily. Kayo varied things a little by sending his ground ball to the shortstop, but he too was out.

The Lions' pitcher was good, Chris thought. He threw harder than the boy who'd pitched for the Colts. Also, he wore a determined expression. Maybe he wouldn't scare so easily.

Pat DeCarlo was pitching for the Bears. Chris didn't dare hope he'd do as well as Kayo had in the first game. Maybe this time everybody would be hitting to right field, to make up for the easy time he'd had before. He had to be ready for anything.

At Mr. Snedecker's signal, Chris moved in a little. In center field Kayo seemed nervous, his face even more solemn than usual.

The Lions' first hitter picked out a bat, walked halfway to the plate, and then walked back and exchanged it for another. He set himself in the box, backed out and bent to tighten a shoelace.

To Chris, waiting in his half-crouched position, each second seemed endless. Just as in the first game, the bits of advice he'd heard in practice crowded into his mind and mixed together in confusion. It was impossible to sort them out. He'd never be able to choose the advice he needed if something happened.

By the time Pat let go his first pitch, Chris had felt his muscles stiffen and his joints lock immovably. He stood as if his feet were glued to the ground, while the Lion batters went down in order—second to first, then a strikeout, then third to first.

He came in, weak with relief that an inning had passed with nothing hit to right field. But Mr. Snedecker approached him, an exasperated look on his face. "My goodness, boy!" he cried, "Can't you remember anything? Why didn't you back up first base on those two plays? Suppose one of those throws had gotten by Howie?"

Chris's face grew hot. "I—I'm sorry, sir," he said weakly. This was what he'd been afraid of. With so many things buzzing in his head, the only one he'd needed had escaped him.

Jerry banged out a solid two-bagger and scored when Pat bounced one over the fence for a ground-rule double. Howie Jennings, the first baseman, sacrificed Pat to third. The order had come around to Chris.

Gripping the bat painfully tight and inwardly trembling with dread, Chris made his way to the plate. As he waited for the first pitch, he saw that the outfielders had moved back to the fence. Then he remembered those balls he'd driven over that fence in practice.

The first pitch whipped in fast, over the plate and barely too low. This pitcher wasn't giving anything away. He was trying hard to get him out, while not putting the ball where it would be too easy to get hold of. The next narrowly missed the outside corner.

The next pitch was too good to hold off on. Chris managed to swing. He missed. But there were gasps from the crowd. A voice said, "Wow! If that had connected—"

Another pitch came in too low, and then another. Chris had himself another walk. Standing at first, he breathed deeply and waited for the fluttering in his stomach to subside.

Mark Ramsey was up next. He seemed to be wasting time—rubbing dirt on his hands, readjusting his helmet. Then Chris heard Mr. Snedecker yelling his name and remembered to look at him. He was mopping his forehead with his handkerchief.

For a moment Chris's mind was blank. Then he

remembered. It was the signal to run with the first pitch. He pretended to brush dust off his pants leg, meaning that he understood.

Mark swung and missed. As the ball passed the plate, Chris moved toward second. He got a slow start, for his feet seemed made of lead. But, as Mr. Snedecker had planned, the Lions' catcher threw to second. Chris was out, but Pat was off like a streak to slide across the plate with the second run. On the next pitch Mark flied out to third.

In the next inning Chris concentrated on backing up first. He was called on to do it twice and both times managed pretty well. Both throws were taken without trouble, but Chris knew it was good practice.

The Lions scored in the bottom of the third, but Chris had nothing to do with that. Pat had loaded the bases with a single to left, a hit batter, and a walk. Then, after two strikeouts, another walk forced in the run.

Chris collected two more walks. Also, he moved in to back up first so many times he was sure he'd never forget again. Pat seemed securely in control of the Lion batters. Though the Bears led by only a single run, that seemed enough.

The Bears took the field for the bottom of the

sixth. Chris told himself that for trouble to come again in the sixth would be like lightning striking twice in the same place. It just couldn't happen. The game was as good as over, and he was still safe in this spot where even a poor player couldn't do much harm.

The first Lion batter went down swinging hard at Pat's fast ball. The second was called out as Pat's curve broke just right. "Only one more," Chris muttered thankfully.

But Pat found that third out hard to get. His curve broke too late on a three-and-two pitch, and the batter was on. Another walk followed, to put runners on first and second.

The left-handed batter at the plate had singled up the middle to lead off the fifth. Chris glanced at Mr. Snedecker, and in response to his signal moved a few steps nearer the foul line.

This time the batter gave him no time to review the situation. He swung at the first pitch, and drove a ground ball hard down the first base line. It was past Howie before he could get his glove down. Chris was positioned perfectly, and needed only a couple of steps to be behind the slowing roller. But his feet seemed rooted to the ground. He moved too late. The ball rolled past him, and he had to turn and pursue it. Awkwardly, with fingers that felt stiff as wood, he picked it up. As he turned around, he saw a runner crossing the plate. Another was rounding third. The batter had turned first and was heading for second.

Out of the confusion in Chris's mind, a single phrase popped out—"get the lead runner." He had forgotten that there were already two out and that the batter, halfway between first and second, should make an easy third. He loosed a desperate heave in the direction of home plate.

As he let go the ball, he knew that it was a weak throw that wasted what momentum it had by going too high. Chris saw that Tommy had been waiting to receive it at second. He had to make a desperate dash off the bag to grab it, while Mark ran to cover. But by that time the speedy left-hander was safely on second. Tommy threw to the plate, but the runner from third beat the throw with ease. The Lions had scored two runs to win the game.

Chris wished the ground would open under his feet and make a hole big enough for him to hide in. But he knew it wouldn't. There just wasn't any place to hide a white elephant—not even in right field.

CHAPTER 7

Safe at First

"DON'T YOU WORRY, BOY," Mr. Snedecker said cheerfully. He and Chris were sitting on the bench, while Bob pitched batting practice for the rest of the Bears. "You're not the only one that ever made a bad play. They make 'em every day, even up in the big leagues. That's the way we learn. This one you're so downhearted about wasn't really your fault—it was mine. I knew you didn't get around fast and had a weak arm. Putting you where you were was my mistake."

"Yes, sir." Chris stared gloomily at the dust between his feet. He knew what the manager was trying to say. He was only surprised at the trouble he was taking to say it kindly.

"You see," Mr. Snedecker went on, "when a boy's trying—when we know he's set his heart on something, it's hard to hurt him by taking it away. But in baseball we have to think about the whole team, and not just one, when we decide what to do."

"Honest, Mr. Snedecker," Chris said, "I understand. Most everybody does make mistakes about us—us extra big people. They always expect us to be better than we are. My father says it's hard for them to remember we're just ordinary fellows. So you don't need to worry about hurting my feelings—honest."

Mr. Snedecker's eyes opened wide and his jaw dropped, in a look of utter amazement. Then he broke out laughing. He laughed so loud and so long that Chris began to feel a little angry. No matter how foolish he'd sounded, Mr. Snedecker shouldn't laugh so hard. He'd only meant to be helpful.

At last Mr. Snedecker brought his laughter under control. "My goodness, boy! I guess I'm not good at beating about the bush. My mistake wasn't in picking you or keeping you on the team. It was not playing you where I knew you ought to play. It's not your feelings I was worried about. It was Howie's. Howie Jennings has wanted to play first base ever since he was knee high. He was my reserve first baseman last season. Mighty good one, too. Naturally, he expected to take over the job this year.

I hated to disappoint him. But it seems I under-estimated Howie. He tells me that's where you ought to be."

Now it was Chris's turn to gasp in amazement. "Me, sir?" he cried. "Me play first base? But—but that's one of the most important positions there is. If I can mess things up in right field, I'd never be able to hold down first."

"Now, wait a minute!" Mr. Snedecker frowned. "You think it's hard to mess things up in right field? Maybe you don't get so many plays there, but the ones you get can make a big difference. You got two chances in two games. You handled one right and we won. You blew the other one and we lost. You couldn't be more important than that, no matter where you were playing—now, could you?"

"I guess not," Chris admitted.

"Ever hear the specifications for a perfect first baseman?" Mr. Snedecker asked.

"No, sir."

"Long, lean and left-handed. That's what they say. Now, who could fit that description better than you? It won't be easy to learn a new position in a hurry. But first is where you belong, and it will mean a lot to the team to have you there. Let's get to work."

It was amazing how true Mr. Snedecker's words turned out to be. The confusion and uncertainty that had plagued Chris in the outfield were miraculously gone. Now there was only one thing to think about—that one spot that was first base.

With the great strides his long legs made possible, Chris never needed to be more than two steps away from that vital spot. After they had practiced a while, with Bob hitting the ball to him and the other infielders throwing in all sorts of ways, Chris discovered that his feet could find the bag all by themselves. With his long legs, his tall body and long arms, he could reach a great variety of grounders, bouncers and fly balls without taking his feet from the base at all. And he'd learned a long time ago to hold onto any ball that came within reach of his glove.

Of course there was also some throwing to do, but when he didn't have to worry about where he might have to run to make a catch he had time to plan where he'd have to throw. Every place where he might have to throw the ball would be the same distance away every time. Chris found that he could even manage to get the ball across to third, provided he threw it the instant he got it out of his glove. For some reason, it seemed that the longer he held the ball before he threw it the weaker his arm became.

The Bears' next opponents, the Stags, were rated a tough team. After winning from the Lions, they'd whipped the Tigers by a score of four to one. Chris was to start at first base against the Stags.

This time chunky little Sandy Baker was pitching. He seemed a strange choice against the league-leading team. But his round face wore a confident grin as he took the mound. In Sandy's customary place at third was slim, quiet Pat DeCarlo.

Chris glanced at Tommy. He was playing well toward first. He glanced behind him at Howie. Howie gave him an encouraging grin as he moved a couple of steps closer.

Just as Kayo and Pat had done in their games, Sandy walked the first batter. Chris tried not to think how ridiculous he must look standing beside this slender kid, more than a foot shorter than himself. But he couldn't help it. He could feel his face slowly reddening.

Then came a single into left. The throw went to third, to hold the lead runner at second. There was nothing for Chris to do but stand and watch, while the baserunner was replaced by another a couple of inches taller.

The next batter dropped a hit between Kayo in

center and Bill in left. Kayo made the pickup, and threw all the way to the plate. But the runner slid under the tag to score. Meanwhile the others advanced to third and second. Once more, Chris could only stand and watch.

A run in, two on, nobody out. Chris could hardly believe his eyes when he looked at the mound. Sandy was blowing an enormous bubble of gum, and seemed troubled by nothing except the prospect that it might burst before it reached its maximum size. Having disposed of that, he got the next batter out on three swinging strikes.

Next at bat was the Stags' second baseman. On the first pitch he bunted, a little too hard and into the middle of the diamond. Mark raced in, scooped it up, and after a rapid glance had told him he hadn't a chance of cutting off the run, threw to first. It was a perfect throw, right into Chris's glove as he stood with his foot on the bag. Nothing to it. Yet he couldn't have felt more triumphant.

When another strikeout had retired the Stags—and the Bears prepared for their turn at bat—Chris discovered that he had moved up still another notch, to bat sixth. Progress, all along the line. Not even the fact that the Bears were trailing by two runs could bother him. Somehow, Chris knew this would be a lucky day.

Tommy led off with a single. Pat struck out. Then Mark walked, sending Tommy to second. Kayo took a ball low, then slammed a drive along the left field line and over the fence. But the cheers died away when the umpire called it foul. With disgusted looks, the runners returned to their bases and Kayo to the plate where he finally settled for a walk. Bases loaded. Then Bill, trying hard for a hit, struck out.

The feeling Chris had had at first base, of being in the right place and knowing exactly what to do, suddenly deserted him. There were two outs, and the bases were loaded with runners, whose fates depended on him. Just as before, his face flamed while his insides seemed to turn to ice. He felt his hands tighten on the bat and all his joints and muscles tighten as if they were turned to stone.

The first pitch was low. But then the Stags' pitcher found the plate with a fast ball just above the knee. Chris managed to swing, too late. Twice more the pitch was in the same spot, and twice more he missed.

It seemed to Chris that he had been split into two different people. The one who was playing first base stretched far to his left to grab a bad throw from Sandy and make the final out in the second. He stretched high over his head to grab a line drive for the third out in the fifth. He stretched far to his right to scoop up a grounder for the last out in the sixth. Those were all the things he had a chance to do at first base, and each one he did just right.

But at the plate nothing went right. Twice more he went down swinging, as the Stag pitcher kept whipping the knee-high fast balls across the plate. Meanwhile, the Bears had brought in two runs to tie the score.

After the six regulation innings had ended in a deadlock, both pitchers had to be relieved. The starters had exhausted their weekly limit.

The Bears' new pitcher was Kayo, coming in from center field. He upheld his reputation as the Bears' best by striking out the side in order. For the Stags it was the little second baseman whose bunt had given Chris the chance for his first play.

Chris would be third at bat in the seventh, after Kayo and Bill. Maybe, he thought hopefully, one of them would score and end it before his turn came. Maybe Kayo would even hit another home run.

No such luck. Kayo drove a single up the middle. Bill put one in almost the same spot, but this time the second baseman was behind it. He threw to the shortstop covering, and Kayo was forced.

Only one out this time. Chris took it for granted he'd strike out again. But at least there'd still be a chance for the Bears, with Jerry coming up.

The first pitch looked like a strike. Dutifully but without hope, Chris swung. But instead of the awful feeling of fanning empty air, this time the ball was there—right in the path of his swing. It felt exactly like the balls he'd hit so often in practice. Like them, it soared up and away and disappeared into the treetops beyond the fence.

As Chris circled the bases, he could hear through his dazed disbelief a tumult of cheers and applause. For him, because his home run had won the game.

But—that meant they'd be expecting him to hit more home runs. Didn't they know? Couldn't they tell that it was the sheerest luck? That new little pitcher had put the ball in the perfect spot for him to hit. And it was a safe bet that not even he would ever do that again.

[CHAPTER 8]

Security or Shelter?

IN THE DAYS THAT FOLLOWED, Chris tried to dodge the congratulations. He tried not to see the admiring glances, or to hear the excited voices of younger boys as they pointed him out to their friends. Chris knew he didn't deserve any of this, and he was sure that when people found out they'd been fooled they'd blame him for it.

Still, other games were being played. Soon some other player would attract people's attention and make them forget him.

Then, when Chris arrived home from school on the Tuesday after the game with the Stags, the door flew open before he could reach for the knob. His mother had opened it, her face flushed with excitement. In her hand was a copy of the weekly Millbrook *Journal*.

"Oh, Chris! You must read what it says about

you in the paper. Look!" She pointed to a place on the sports page.

Chris put down his books on the hall table, then took the newspaper and read, "The winning runs scored on a towering home run by Chris Sorensen. The powerful first baseman, a newcomer to Millbrook, blasted what was by a wide margin the longest drive ever seen at the local field. . . ."

"Your father told me you got a good hit," Chris's mother said, "but I had no idea it was *that* good. You know what? I'm going to clip this out and start a scrapbook."

Here was something Chris had never expected. Since Dover Falls was too small to support a newspaper, no reports of their Little League games had found their way into print. Whether you won or lost—became a hero or a goat—was soon forgotten in favor of newer events. But here in Millbrook, everything was set down in black and white. Nothing could ever be really forgotten.

Though he couldn't help feeling proud of what had been said about him, Chris winced at the thought of what would happen. Everybody who read this would be looking at him harder than ever in the next game, expecting him to do something good.

And his mother! She'd buy a big scrapbook and proudly paste in this clipping. Then she'd wait for more—lots more, enough to fill it up.

Besides that, she'd probably buy more papers, to send to their relatives and friends in Dover Falls. Then they'd be waiting, too, expecting wonderful things that he would never do.

It was horrible to think about. But Chris knew that if he told his mother she wouldn't understand.

*　*　*　*　*

When the Bears assembled for their Saturday game with the Tigers, Chris found himself batting fourth. If he'd really earned the right to be in the coveted clean-up spot, he could have felt proud. As it was, he only wondered how long he'd stay there.

This time the Bears were first up. Tommy drew a walk. Then Sandy hit a fly ball to the left fielder. Mark fanned, for the second out.

There was applause as Chris stepped to the plate. They had all read that piece in the newspaper and were expecting him to knock the ball out of the lot. As he stood waiting for the first pitch, Chris felt more frozen with dread than ever before.

But apparently the Tiger pitcher had also read the newspaper. His first two pitches were low, the next two far outside. Another walk for Chris. Kayo singled him to second, while Tommy sped home with the first Bear run. Then Bill's long fly dropped in the center fielder's glove to end the inning.

Once more Chris took his place at first. It was like coming home. Here he felt secure and comfortable, for he knew he could do what was expected of him. Taking a throw from Pat to end the scoreless inning filled him with satisfaction.

As the Bears came to bat in the second, Chris watched from the bench. Jerry struck out. Then Pat hit a high, short fly. It was the kind that could drop in—just inside the foul line—back of first base yet too far in for the right fielder. But the Tiger first baseman raced nimbly back and got under it. Two outs.

Howie kept things going with a walk, and seconds later little Tommy O'Brien amazed everyone with a drive that just cleared the fence and brought in two runs.

Then it was Sandy's turn. Chris watched with envy and amazement. As usual, Sandy was chewing away on a wad of bubble gum. As usual, it seemed that he couldn't care less about anything except completing one last, perfect bubble before he took his place at the plate. Chris would have given anything to be so much at ease.

The count on Sandy reached three-and-two, and the chubby third baseman was as nonchalant as ever. He guarded the plate, managing somehow to get his bat on every pitch that came over it. Four in a row he fouled away, fending off the strikeout. The fifth pitch was again hit foul and headed for the bleachers on the first-base side. But the Tigers' first baseman raced after it. Just inside the fence he leaped, grabbed, and held the ball for the third out.

During the rest of the game Chris had eyes only for that Tiger first baseman. He had none of the qualities Mr. Snedecker had said a first baseman needed. He was rather short, a bit pudgy, and right-handed. But he ranged boldly over a wide territory, accepting chances Chris would never have imagined trying for.

As he watched, Chris pictured how he must look as he played his position. Perhaps he looked as if he had one foot chained to the bag, and with a mighty short chain, at that. Yet he was playing just as Mr. Snedecker had told him to, and just as his teammates seemed to expect.

As he compared the Tiger defense to that of the Bears, Chris began to feel deeply humiliated. He realized that Tommy played far toward first, while Mark in turn played close to second and Sandy wide of third. Howie was stationed close in to back him up. Jerry raced far up the line to field foul flies he should have taken. And the pitcher came off the mound to field bunts that should have been his responsibility.

The fact was, Chris told himself, he wasn't a first baseman at all. At best, he was only half a first baseman. All the rest of the team was working together to make up for his shortcomings. What Mr. Snedecker had given him wasn't the security of a job he could do well. It was just a shelter.

But why would the rest of the team cover up for him this way? Not because they liked him, that was sure. They were friendly enough on the field, but not one had ever seemed to want his company away from it. They did like Mr. Snedecker though. They'd do anything for him.

But then, why would a smart manager like Mr. Snedecker ask his team to do such a thing? Why would he insist that they carry a white elephant on their backs while they played? It just didn't make sense, unless—

Of course! He'd almost forgotten that Mr. Snedecker was looking ahead to football, and the help the Big Swede could give him in organizing a Millbrook league.

At last the game ended. The Bears had beaten the Tigers six to one, to take first place in the league. But Chris was so absorbed in thoughts of his own inadequacy that he hardly cared.

After the game, he hung around till everyone else had gone. He had made up his mind to tell Mr. Snedecker he was on the wrong track. His father wouldn't be influenced by the way his son was treated, he would say. And so Mr. Snedecker had better drop him to the minors while he still could—before the first round of games was over.

But, at the last instant, Chris's nerve failed. He only stammered out a question about the next practice and hurried away.

After all, Chris told himself, it was his father he should talk to. He'd tell his father the story and ask him to talk to Mr. Snedecker. If his father would either promise or refuse right now, making it clear that what happened to his son wouldn't change his mind, then Mr. Snedecker could be free to do what he wanted. Then, if he stayed on the Bears, he'd know it was because Mr. Snedecker thought he deserved to.

Later, while his mother was putting the girls to bed, Chris's father gave him a perfect chance. "How'd the game go?" he asked. "Sorry I couldn't get away from work in time to see it. I like the way Mr. Snedecker handles his team. He strikes me as a fine man, Chris. You're lucky to have him for a manager."

With that, the words Chris had so carefully rehearsed stuck in his throat. He realized that if he said them he'd be accusing Mr. Snedecker of being far different from the fine man his father and everybody else thought he was. He'd be saying Mr. Snedecker was using deception and favoritism to try to buy something he wanted. That would be terrible, even if he were one hundred percent sure he was right.

So he only said, "You didn't miss much. We beat 'em six to one. Sandy Baker pitched—did a good job. Tommy O'Brien hit a home run."

"Well! I can see you've got a fine team." Chris's father smiled, nodded, and reached for the book he'd been reading. He hadn't thought to ask what Chris had done. Or else he was being tactful.

CHAPTER 9

Welcome from a Wildcat

TROUBLE SEEMS TWICE AS BAD when you can't talk about it. And there was no one Chris could talk to. Not his parents, nor Mr. Snedecker. Not his sisters. They were too young. And he'd made no close friends at his new school. Least of all could he talk to his teammates of the Bears. He was sure they must hate him for being Mr. Snedecker's pet white elephant. Chris couldn't blame them. If he were in their shoes, he'd feel the same way.

In desperation, he sat down to write a letter to Ricky Thompson, his best friend in Dover Falls. He meant to tell Ricky everything, just as if they were talking. But the minute he started trying to put down what had been happening and the way he felt, he knew it wouldn't work.

He could almost hear Ricky's scornful voice. "So—

you're playing first base for a hotshot team. Already you've hit the longest home run in history. And you tell me you've got troubles?"

Chris tore up what he'd written and started again. This time he wrote just the usual news about the weather, school, and his family. He didn't mention baseball.

There was nothing to do but keep his worries to himself. To make things worse, in a few days school would be out. Everybody else was so happy they could hardly wait. But all it meant to Chris was long, empty days with nothing to do but cut the grass, weed the flower bed, run a few errands for his mother—and play baseball. Nothing to take his mind away from his awful predicament.

The game with the Wildcats was on the Saturday following the last day of school. Chris's father was there, perched on the top row of the bleachers. Chris tried not to look at him, but he couldn't forget he was there.

He hoped this would be an easy game, so nothing he did would be very important. The Wildcats had two wins on their record, but one was over the cellar team, the Colts. In the other their top pitcher had faced the Stags' third-string hurler, and still it had been close.

Once again the Bears were first at bat. This time Chris was second in the order. After five games, Mr. Snedecker still didn't know where to put him. Each time, he reshuffled the batting order. Nobody complained, but Chris knew everybody must resent the confusion and blame him.

The Wildcats' pitcher was a plump, placid-looking boy with a faceful of freckles and a toothy grin. Their catcher—Chris blinked in disbelief. That kid couldn't *really* be their catcher. Though he was decked out in mask, shin guards and chest protector, he must be just helping with the warmup. Crouched behind the plate, he looked about the size of a cricket. And when he straightened up to toss the ball to the mound it was easy to see that Tommy, the smallest of the Bears who now approached the plate, towered over him by several inches.

But when the first pitch came over for a called strike on Tommy, there was no more room for doubt. The little boy, who was not only short but so skinny he didn't begin to fill up the uniform with number one on the back, was really the Wildcats' catcher.

Tommy bounced one to the mound for an easy out at first. Chris stepped to the plate.

If anything could have made him feel more conspicuous than usual, it was that tiny catcher. Besides, the thought of that frail handful of skin and bones crouched so close behind him turned his self-conscious stiffness into absolute paralysis. Suppose his bat should slip? Even a glancing blow would probably kill a kid that size. There was hardly anything to him. For a moment Chris even pictured the little catcher floating through the air, blown like a handful of feathers by the wind from a healthy swing.

But luck was with Chris. The Wildcat pitcher, suddenly cautious, missed the plate four times in a row. Chris had added another walk to his already large collection.

Then, his teeth once more gleaming in a confident smile, the freckled boy settled down to strike out first Jerry and then Kayo to retire the side.

Chris took his place at first. Kayo was on the mound, with Pat in center field and the others in their usual positions.

The first Wildcat batter, the shortstop, drew a walk. Following him in the number two spot—the spot that equaled Chris's own in the Bears' lineup—was that diminutive catcher.

Now that the kid no longer wore his catcher's gear, Chris could get a better look. There was something frail and babyish about him that made it hard to believe he was old enough to belong on the field. He looked as if he'd be at home in the first grade.

Applause swelled from the bleachers. There were whistles, and voices calling encouragement. "Yeah, Hobie!" "Come on, Hobie—show 'em how to hit that ball!"

Hobie—so that was the kid's name. Chris had never heard of anyone being called that before.

Hobie smiled and nodded at the crowd, like an actor taking a bow. Then he stepped to the plate and crouched, his bat held well back, a look of fierce determination on his face.

"Looking for a walk," Chris muttered. "He's too short to pitch to."

The Wildcats' shortstop grinned, as he took a step off the bag. "I wouldn't bet on that," he said.

Hobie swung hard, and sent a foul soaring over the backstop. He swung again at the next pitch. This time he hit a sizzling drive past Tommy's diving stab. It went into right field for a single, and advanced the runner to third.

With one tiny foot on the bag, Hobie grinned up at Chris. "How's the weather up there, pal?" he asked.

"Okay," Chris mumbled. More than ever before, he felt clumsy and enormous. To see this puny specimen hit the ball when he couldn't was more humiliating than anything else that had happened. To make things worse, he knew that if he'd been a real first baseman he'd at least have tried to stop that ball instead of leaving it for Tommy.

As the next batter stepped to the plate, Hobie edged far off the bag. But as Kayo threw to Chris, he was back just in time. Off he went again. Another throw, and another quick return.

At last Kayo toed the rubber and threw. The batter popped it up in front of the plate, and Jerry gathered it in. One out. Both runners held their bases.

Again Hobie began his game of edging far off base, then diving back at the last instant. Chris felt like an elephant being tormented by a mouse.

Another batter popped up to the mound, and there were two outs. One more and he'd be rid of this little pest, Chris told himself thankfully.

Then, as Kayo put his first pitch across the plate, Hobie took off and kept going. Jerry whipped a strike to Tommy at second, and Hobie headed back to first. Tommy's throw to Chris was hard and poorly aimed. Chris had to go a couple of steps behind the bag to grab it, and as he turned he saw Hobie sprawled on the ground, a look of agony on his baby face.

"My ankle!" It was a faint, high-pitched cry, like the squeak of a suffering mouse.

Chris bent over the tiny boy, forgetting everything in concern for his injury. "Just take it easy," he said, "I'll—" But before he could get another word out of his mouth the prostrate figure lunged, rolled, twisted, and had a hand solidly on the bag. The umpire gestured with palms down—safe.

Chris's jaw dropped. He stared in helpless bewilderment and dismay. He'd never argued with an umpire in his life, but this was too much. "But, sir! He was hurt. I didn't think he could move."

The umpire, a stocky man hardly taller than Mr. Snedecker, craned his neck to look Chris in the eye. He snapped, "Runner's safe!" Then he bent over Hobie. "You hurt, kid?"

"Hurt? No, sir. Not me." Hobie sprang briskly to his feet and brushed dust from his uniform.

There was laughter from the bleachers, and then loud applause. While Chris had stood holding the ball, the runner from third had crossed the plate. Jerry was glaring toward first, red-faced with fury. Too late, Chris remembered a voice shouting his name and knew it had been Jerry's.

Chris tossed the ball to Kayo. He wished he could sneak away and disappear. He'd never set foot on a baseball diamond again.

As Kayo prepared to pitch to the next batter, the umpire spoke to Chris again. This time his tone was friendly. "Next time you think somebody's hurt, son, put the tag on him and then call time. If you don't, the ball's in play."

Chris nodded and mumbled thanks. Then, before he knew it, there was the ball driven along the ground right at him. He reached down, missed, and saw it roll between his feet. Howie missed it, too, then turned and chased it nearly to the fence. By the time he picked it up, Hobie was flying toward third. By the time the throw came to Tommy and was relayed to the plate, Hobie had slid across to score the second run.

After that the game became a pitchers' battle, with neither team able to score. The Wildcats won it, two to nothing.

Afterward there was a strained, unnatural silence, as if everybody were so busy remembering not to mention Chris's blunders that they didn't have time to think of anything else.

As he walked toward the car where his father waited, Chris felt like crying with misery and loneliness. But of course he was much too big to do that.

Then there was the sound of running steps behind him. A high-pitched voice called breathlessly, "Hey! Wait a minute."

Chris turned around. It was Hobie. His blue eyes were beaming friendliness, and on his face was a radiant smile. "Your name's Chris, right? Chris Sorensen? Mine's Hobie Timmons. I was just thinking—are you going to the flicks tonight?"

"Flicks?" Chris shook a puzzled head.

"You know—the movies. Everybody goes Saturdays, to the early show at the Palace, but I never see you there. How about giving it a try tonight? Meet me outside about a quarter to seven?"

"Oh—well—sure, I'd like to." Chris had been hating Hobie since that first inning, for playing a dirty trick on him. But here was Hobie, friendly as a pup and obviously not feeling a bit guilty. So maybe it had all been an accident—a misunderstanding. It must have been because here was Hobie giving him his first real welcome to Millbrook.

In an instant Chris's loneliness had vanished, and with it most of his misery. Suddenly he felt light and free, and intensely grateful to the boy who had made the feeling possible. He knew Hobie Timmons was the nicest kid he'd ever met.

[CHAPTER 10]

Everybody Goes There

THE MINUTE CHRIS ACCEPTED Hobie's invitation, he knew he shouldn't have. Not without asking his father. He'd never been to a movie without his parents. Among the many things which Dover Falls was too small to support was a movie theater. The nearest one was at Hillcrest, ten miles away. Dover Falls boys and girls went to the movies with their parents, or they didn't go. Chris had no idea what his parents would think of his going with just a bunch of boys. But he made up his mind to argue, coax, or even beg on his knees—whatever he had to do to get permission.

But, to Chris's surprise, his father didn't seem to mind. He handed over a crisp dollar bill and said to call if he wanted a ride home. Even his mother didn't really object. She only said it seemed odd to plan going to the movies when he didn't know what was playing.

"It must be something good," Chris argued, "or why would everybody's parents let them go?"

At that his mother laughed and said, "I give up!"

Chris whistled cheerfully as he walked toward the center of town. It was the first time he'd felt in a whistling mood since he'd moved to Millbrook. But suddenly, in spite of the awfulness of this afternoon's game, things seemed to be going his way.

Having a friend in Millbrook made all the difference. Especially when the friend was a great kid like Hobie. To be so small, and yet to play baseball the way Hobie did, made a kid something special. Chris remembered the way people had cheered and called Hobie's name when he came to bat. With Hobie as a friend, Chris could become part of what the kids meant when they said "everybody."

As Chris approached the theater, he saw that the sidewalk was already jammed with kids. The air was filled with the sound of their voices, their laughter, their feet scuffling on cement. Chris guessed the youngest ones were about nine, the oldest about sixteen.

He stopped a couple of doors away and pretended to study the pictures of houses for sale in the window of a real estate office. Out of the corner of his eye he searched the crowd for Hobie. He couldn't see him. He did see Sandy and Mark and Pat, standing near the ticket window. But they didn't see him, and he stepped farther back in the doorway so they wouldn't.

Time crept by. The line grew longer and more noisy. Still, Hobie didn't appear. The ticket window opened, and the line began to move forward. Still no Hobie.

Chris's happy mood faded. As the end of the line inched into the lobby, he was struck by a horrible thought. Suppose Hobie had been playing a trick on him? After a few minutes Chris was convinced that was true. Of course! How could he have believed that, after nobody in Millbrook had paid any attention to him in all these weeks, a kid like Hobie would suddenly adopt him as a friend? Chris felt his face redden, as he imagined Hobie and his friends watching from some hidden spot, laughing at how easily he'd been fooled. He turned on his heel, resolved to go home and try to forget it.

"Hey, Chris!" Hobie's breathless treble stopped him short. In shorts and a summer shirt that left his skinny legs and frail-looking arms bare, he appeared even more tiny. "Sorry I kept you waiting."

"That's all right." Seeing Hobie's pinched little face looking so apologetic, Chris was ashamed of his suspicions.

He followed Hobie to the ticket window. The sign said: CHILDREN TWELVE AND UNDER, 50¢. ADULTS, $1.25. That was higher than the prices of the movie house in Hillcrest. Still, he'd be all right. He had a whole dollar.

Hobie reached up and put a half-dollar on the counter. The woman slid a blue ticket across to him.

Chris put down his dollar. The woman just looked at him. "One child's ticket, please," Chris said.

The woman frowned, pursed her lips, and glared at him. "You kidding? That'll be a dollar and a quarter."

"But—" If Chris had had a quarter he would have paid it gladly. If he'd been alone he'd have given up and gone home. "But, ma'am, I won't be thirteen till October," he said earnestly.

The woman shook her head. "You kids! I pass 'em in here thirteen, fourteen—maybe older if they're small. Figure maybe they *could* be telling the truth. But when a big fellow, must be six feet tall, tries it—I draw the line at being taken for a fool."

Chris looked appealingly at Hobie, and saw that he was shaking with silent laughter. But after a moment he stepped to Chris's side. "It's—it's true, ma'am. He really is—honest—only twelve." But Hobie's words were so mingled with giggles that even to Chris they sounded unconvincing.

More kids were lining up behind them. They stared at Chris, exchanging whispered remarks and skeptical laughter. Even people passing by turned to stare. Chris felt that in one more minute he would die of embarrassment.

Then he felt a hand on his arm, and heard a familiar voice. "What's the trouble here?"

"Oh, Mr. Snedecker! Good evening." The woman smiled brightly. "This young fellow's trying to tell me he's only twelve."

Mr. Snedecker smiled back at her. "Know just how you feel, Mrs. Sharp. Chris here walked up to me one day and told me that. I didn't believe him, either. But he happened to have his birth certificate along. Had to believe that, didn't I? Yes, ma'am! He's one of my Little League boys."

"Well—I never—" Mrs. Sharp looked flustered as she handed Chris his ticket and his change. "Lucky you came along, Mr. Snedecker. I'd never have believed it. Chris, I'm sorry. But don't you worry about coming back. I'll remember you next time."

Inside, Hobie stopped at a candy machine and bought several boxes of hard candies. He gave a couple to Chris and stuck the rest in his pocket.

"Thanks, Hobie," Chris said.

"Don't mention it."

Hobie led the way up to the balcony. The newsreel had just started, and by the dim light Chris saw that nearly all the seats were filled. What he could see of downstairs looked almost empty. Only a few grownups were scattered among the expanse of seats.

Hobie spotted a couple of empty seats in a row of boys, and headed for them. But Pat, on the end, barred the way. "Cut it out, Hobie. We're saving those." The same thing happened again, with a boy Chris didn't know. At last they found seats in the middle of an empty row.

Chris loved movies. Each time he went, he lost himself in a magic world, and afterward he enjoyed remembering what he'd seen. He had a little trouble drifting into the jungle world of this movie. There was too much noise—kids whispering, giggling, rattling candy wrappers and popcorn bags. But after a few minutes the distractions were forgotten. He was thousands of miles away, on the trail of a man-eating tiger. Once in a while, automatically, he reached into his pocket for one of the candies Hobie had given him, and popped it into his mouth.

Suddenly something touched his shoulder. Could it be some jungle beast, or one of those fat snakes that hung from the trees? Chris's panicky start took his right out of his seat. Then he saw that it was only an usher.

"All right, wise guy," the usher said grimly, "out you go."

"Huh? Out? Why?" Chris, his mind still half in the jungle, groped for reality.

"You know why! Out! Or do I have to call a cop?" The usher pulled at his arm.

"Just a minute." Hobie was gazing at the screen, wide-eyed and oblivious as someone in a trance. Chris hated to disturb him, but it had to be done. He tapped his shoulder and whispered, "Hobie! I'll wait for you outside."

Hobie blinked in apparent bewilderment, then said, "Oh! All right," and returned to his trance.

As he left, Chris tried once more. "I didn't do anything."

"Sure! Always innocent!" the usher scoffed. "Knocked that lady's hat right off. Could've put her eye out if she'd happened to turn around. Any of you punks ever think about that, huh?"

"I wasn't near any lady," Chris protested.

"Next you'll tell me you didn't have any candy."

"Candy?"

"Yeah, candy!" With a sudden pounce, the usher slid his hand into Chris's pocket and pulled out a half-empty box. "A piece just like this is what knocked the lady's hat off. You might as well throw a rock."

It was no use arguing. The usher had made a mistake, but there was no way to prove it. Meekly, Chris went outside. Once more he lurked in the doorway. He'd have a long wait before the movie was over and Hobie came out. But it was darker, and fewer people were passing. Maybe nobody would notice him.

At last the doors opened, and the crowd swarmed out. Chris spotted Hobie and greeted him with a sheepish grin. When he'd explained, Hobie shook his head and said, "That's really tough, Chris. What say we stop at the Shack for a hamburger? Everybody goes there."

The Shack was small, filled to overflowing with the smell of frying hamburgers and the loud music of a juke box. The customers packed tightly into it seemed of high-school age. Not one was as young as Chris and Hobie.

Chris hung back, but Hobie dived between two bigger boys and headed for the counter. "Come on," he called, "there's two just leaving."

Chris wanted only to eat his hamburger and leave. From the talk that flew back and forth between the groups of older kids, the familiar nicknames and the private jokes they exchanged, it was plain they all knew each other well. Chris felt like an intruder in a private club.

They were served quickly. Chris gulped down his hamburger, hardly tasting it. But Hobie dawdled over his. Chris fidgeted impatiently, and tried to ease the waiting by reading the posters on the wall.

There was a startled yelp in his ear. Then a resounding thud. Chris whirled, and saw a large boy in a vividly patterned sport shirt sprawled on the floor at his feet. He leaped from his stool to help.

But the older boy was already on his feet. He looked enormous—several inches taller than Chris and at least twice as broad. He grabbed Chris's shirt front in a powerful hand and swung the other fist to within a hairsbreadth of Chris's nose.

"Trip me up, will you?" he demanded. "Tired of living, bud?"

Astonishment and terror turned Chris's bones to jelly and his blood to ice water. His voice came out faint and trembly. "But I didn't! I—Look there, that must have been what did it." In a desperate attempt to escape blame, he pointed to a worn patch in the linoleum where a small piece curled up.

The big boy didn't bother to look. "When I can't tell a bump in the floor from somebody's foot, I'll quit! Now, let's step out back and see if you can do that again when I'm looking for it."

Chris shook his head and tried to pull away.

"What's the matter, big shot? You're not *scared?*"

"Course he's not scared! Everybody knows you can't get out of your own way, Lard Barrel!" Chris had thought nothing could scare him more than he already was. But Hobie's taunting voice did it. This big guy would really kill him now.

But, amazingly, the grip on his shirt front relaxed. Slowly, the determined fury on the pudgy face turned to helpless fury. "All right," the big boy said softly. "Let's just forget it. I guess you're new around here, so I'll give you a little advice. Be careful of the company you keep. Get it?"

"Sure—sure—I get it." Chris nodded an emphatic assent, and escaped.

He got it, all right. And he wouldn't forget it. Nobody would catch him trying to mingle with the high school crowd at the Shack. Never again!

CHAPTER 11

Alias the Holy Terror

FOR THE NEXT FEW DAYS Chris stayed close to home. He cut the grass and weeded the flower beds without being told. He cleaned the cellar and the garage, washed the windows, and even volunteered to stay with his little sisters while his mother went shopping.

Though at first she was delighted, it wasn't long before Chris's mother began to look at him with suspicion, and then with alarm. On Tuesday, when for the fiftieth time he asked if there wasn't something he could do to help, she threw up her hands with a look of amused desperation.

"Honestly, Chris! You've done more work in a few days than you usually do in a month. This is vacation, dear! Why don't you go out and have some fun?"

Chris frowned. "Nothing to do around here."

"Of course there's nothing to do if you just stay home. At least, you could go for a walk. Or—why don't you call that boy you went to the movies with the other night? Invite him over, or see if he has any ideas?"

Chris shook his head. He hadn't told his mother about what had happened the night when he and Hobie went to the movies, and he hoped she wouldn't hear. It would be hard for her to believe he hadn't done anything to bring so much trouble on himself. But, since he hadn't told her, he couldn't expect her to understand why calling Hobie was out of the question. Hobie had stuck with him through that awful evening, but it wouldn't be fair to expect him to risk anything like it again.

"I'll just rest," he said. "We've got a game to-night."

Once in his room, Chris found himself wishing that he were back in Dover Falls. He hadn't done that for quite a while. Being first baseman for the Bears, even getting his name in the local paper after that lucky home run, had seemed to offer a chance of belonging in Millbrook. But it had been Hobie's friendliness that had let him feel, for a little while, that Millbrook was no longer a strange town but a new home.

Saturday night had proved that feeling wrong. Millbrook wasn't home. It wasn't just a bigger Dover Falls, with fun and friends waiting to be discovered. It was a nightmare place, where people accused and threatened without reason, and there was no telling what dreadful thing would happen next.

It was strange to remember that a few weeks ago he'd thought the biggest difference between Dover Falls and Millbrook was the way they played baseball. Now it seemed that baseball was the only thing in a confusing world that stayed the same.

Tonight's game started the second round of play. The Bears faced the Colts—the cellar team with only one victory to their credit. But, Chris remembered, the Bears hadn't beaten the Colts easily in their first game. That lucky catch of his had come just at the right time. Maybe this time he'd be lucky again.

But that was just the trouble. The few times he'd done something to help the Bears had been pure luck. The errors, the blunders, and failures had been his own with no luck involved. He couldn't expect luck to save him forever. And, even if he could, he wouldn't want to. He wanted to earn his place on the team by his ability, not by his size or by his father's reputation. And he needed to know that the crowd's applause was for something he'd done, not just for something lucky that had happened to him.

Chris wasn't surprised that he had slipped to seventh in the batting order. That was natural enough, after the mess he'd made of things in the last game.

Sandy was pitching, and chewing bubble gum as nonchalantly as ever. The first batter drove a ground ball in Chris's direction, and Chris stretched to scoop it up with his foot on the bag for the first out. The next batter walked, only to be forced at second when Pat grabbed another grounder off third and got off a nice peg to Tommy. The inning ended when the Colts' cleanup hitter struck out.

It was that same cleanup hitter who turned out to be the Colts' pitcher. Chris saw that he threw the ball in almost exactly the same place every time. But he did throw very fast so that the batters hurried their swings. Tommy bounced to the shortstop and was out at first. Pat popped up to first, and Mark to third, and that ended the inning.

Sandy struck out three Colts' batters in a row for a quick top of the second, and the Bears were ready for their second chance. Kayo popped to second and Jerry to first. But this time the Colts' first base-man fumbled what should have been an easy chance, and Jerry was safe. That brought up Sandy, who struck out.

No use hoping for a walk this time, Chris thought. This kid hadn't missed the plate more than twice in pitching to six batters. And he didn't seem even to notice who the batter was—just stood and threw as hard as he could. Nothing to do but get ready to swing away.

Swing away he did. And, for the second time in a game, Chris had the thrilling realization that the ball was there. Just right. Just—exactly—right! This time he didn't stand at the plate paralyzed with amazement before he started to run. This time he ran, but he didn't hurry. Even if he hadn't seen the ball clear the fence still rising, he would have known from the instant of silence followed by the chorus of cheers, that he'd hit another home run. Jerry scored ahead of him, and the Bears led two to nothing.

"Boy, oh *boy*, Chris!" Kayo grinned broadly as he pounded Chris on the back. The game was over. The Bears had won again, this time by a score of five to three. "You know that was a longer hit than the one you got before, against the Stags? I can't wait to see what they're going to say about you in the paper this time."

Chris shook his head, mumbled, "I was just lucky," and moved to escape. But Kayo held tenaciously to his arm.

"Come on," he insisted, "you're going our way. You live over on Elm, not far from our house. Tell you what I'll do. I'll treat you and the shrimp to an ice cream."

"No—I can't believe it!" Kayo's little brother Tommy staggered, wide-eyed and open-mouthed. He seemed on the verge of collapse from sheer astonishment. "Chris, you better take that ice cream while you've got a chance. This tightwad will never offer you one again."

"Shut up, half-pint," Kayo said amiably. "When's the last time you hung onto enough money to treat anybody?"

Boys and girls were lined up at the ice cream truck. While Chris and Kayo waited, Tommy swung an imaginary bat. "Pow! Pow! Pow!" he shouted triumphantly with each swing. "They'll never find that ol' ball! It's still going, boy! You got the range now, Chris. From now on those other teams might as well give up."

Chris was glad when he could take his ice cream

and hurry away. Everybody was looking at him. "You forgot to mention I struck out my other two times at bat," he told Tommy grimly.

"That's all right," Tommy chortled. "One home run a game will do for a start."

At last Kayo seemed to notice Chris's embarrassment. He said, "All right, pipsqueak. Quiet down and eat the ice cream."

For a few minutes the three walked along in silence. Then Kayo glanced uneasily at Chris. "I hear you had some trouble Saturday."

Chris nodded. News surely got around. He hoped it wouldn't get far enough to reach his parents. "But I didn't do anything, Kayo, honest."

He'd expected scornful disbelief. Instead, Kayo nodded agreement. "But somebody threw that candy. Somebody tripped that big guy in the Shack."

"Well—I guess so. But I don't know who. Or why they should blame me."

"You don't?" Kayo's tone was skeptical.

"No, of course I don't. I—I suppose you mean Hobie did it. Just because he was sitting with me. But he didn't. He's a nice kid."

"He is?"

"Sure he is," Chris insisted. "Everybody likes

Hobie. You can tell that by the way they cheer when he comes to bat."

"The way who cheers? Not kids. Just parents. Parents think Hobie is 'just too sweet.' They think H. T. stands for *Hero* Timmons. But we know it stands for Holy Terror. We steer clear of him, because anybody that hangs around with Hobie is looking for trouble."

Chris stopped short and glared at Kayo. "I don't believe you. You've got it in for Hobie, so you want everybody else to hate him, too. Or maybe you hate me, so you don't want me to have even one friend. But Hobie's the only kid in Millbrook that's been nice to me. I think he's a great guy. You can't make me believe anything bad about him." And Chris stalked angrily away.

But no matter how fast he walked, he couldn't help hearing Kayo saying, "All right. It's your funeral, Chris. Just don't say I didn't warn you."

CHAPTER 12

The One Sure Thing

THE NEXT ISSUE of the Millbrook *Journal* contained a glowing description of Chris and his home run against the Colts. It ended on a note of breathless enthusiasm, "Officials who measured the big Swede's drive declare it may be an all-time record for distance hit by a Little Leaguer."

Chris gulped, and hastily reread the article. No mention of his father. It must be just coincidence that they'd called him "the big Swede." It was a natural enough nickname for a boy whose name was Sorensen and who was nearly six feet tall. But Chris wished whoever had written the piece hadn't thought of it.

At the Bears' next game, the crowd was unusually large. Chris told himself that was just because the game was against the Lions, a pretty good team.

But it seemed to him that all the people were watching him.

When play began, he found he hadn't just imagined that. There was applause when he took the field, and each time he came to the plate voices screamed to him to hit another home run, an even longer one.

It was the hottest day of the season. The sun was a burning glare, like a huge bright lamp focused on Chris, pinning him down in its merciless light so everyone could stare at him. More than ever, he felt huge and stiff and clumsy. He was sure his miserable self-consciousness would make him do something disgracefully awkward and stupid, something that would change the cheers to laughter.

Yet he didn't. Kayo pitched better than ever before. First base was quiet, with only a few easy plays coming his way.

The Lions' pitcher was the one who'd worked the first game. He'd walked Chris three times then, and today he repeated the performance. He even let Chris rack up an RBI, when after hits by Bill, Tommy and Pat had loaded the bases, he dared not put the ball within Chris's reach. The final score was a five to nothing victory for the Bears.

Hobie was waiting for Chris after the game. "You

sure got 'em scared!" he cried happily. "No wonder, after all that stuff in the paper. Suppose it really was a record—that last home run?"

Chris shrugged, and walked a little faster. Hobie's clear, breathless treble carried amazingly. Chris could see the Lions' pitcher and a couple of his friends looking resentfully in his direction. He didn't blame them. It must be bad enough to be shut out in a game, without having to hear the opinion broadcast that they'd been scared out of it.

When they had outdistanced the others, with Hobie trotting to keep pace with Chris's long strides, Chris said impatiently, "What's the difference? Why make such a big deal out of it? A home run counts just as much if it's barely over the fence as if it goes a mile."

"Sure," Hobie said, grinning. "And a *run* counts just as much no matter how you get it. But you don't see pitchers scared green of guys that hit singles. The home-run hitter's the hero, boy. And the longer the home run, the bigger hero he is. What's the use worrying about whether it ought to be that way. You're a hero, so enjoy it!"

Part of the time Chris did enjoy it. He couldn't help being thrilled at the admiring looks, or at the cheers and applause—at least, until he tightened up with dread as he remembered he could never do what everybody was waiting for.

Then came Saturday's game against the Stags. Each time Chris stepped to the plate, the crowd screamed, "Come on, Swede! You can do it!"

Chris could hardly keep himself from throwing down the bat and shouting back at them, "But I can't! I never could—I was just lucky."

And he couldn't and didn't. The best he could do was another base on balls, sandwiched between two strikeouts. The Bears won again anyway, as everybody else managed to get at least one hit.

Afterward, riding home, Chris's father said, "I'm no baseball man, Chris. But, seems to me you're all tightened up. There's no game you can play when you're that way."

Chris scowled, slumping down in the seat. "Just because I didn't get a hit, you don't have to pick on me."

His father gave him a surprised glance. "I didn't mean it that way, son. I've told you before, people expect too much of us big fellows. Maybe you're letting that scare you. Can't you just figure you're out there for fun? Relax and play your game. Don't think you have to hit a home run every time."

"I'll try."

But, when the time came in their game against the Tigers, he just couldn't do it. Four times Chris came to bat. Four times he struck out swinging, as the Tiger pitcher kept the ball low. Each time the fans shouted that he could do it. But by the fourth time, when with two out in the extra eighth inning, Chris struck out to leave the winning runs stranded on the bases and give the Tigers a four to three victory, the voices sounded almost angry. They seemed to think he could hit a home run any time, and was simply refusing to.

As the boys straggled dejectedly from the field, Mr. Snedecker motioned to Chris to remain. Wearily, Chris slumped on the bench beside the manager. Now that the game was over, he felt limp as a rag doll, and every part of him ached.

"Maybe you don't want to admit you made a mistake," he accused Mr. Snedecker. "You won't have to. Just let me quit."

"My goodness, boy!" Mr. Snedecker snapped. "Will you listen to me a minute? You've made up your mind I picked you just because you were big. Or just because your father was a famous football player. Or just because—anything but the real reason. Which was, that I saw the makings of a good baseball player."

"But you said yourself I was a white elephant," Chris objected.

"Oh, that! Sure, I said that. Didn't intend for you to hear, but afterward I was afraid you had. Why, Chris, I say worse things than that all the time, about everybody. My old boys don't mind. They know it's just my way of blowing off steam. At the time, I couldn't figure out where I'd fit you in my lineup. But I was bound I'd fit you in somewhere."

"Why?" Chris demanded.

"Why? Because potentially you're one of the best hitters I ever saw. Good eye. Nice, level swing. Lots of power. Not many players start with so many things going for them. Just remember that. All you need's a little more confidence, so you can loosen up and play the way you ought to play. Won't you try to do that, Chris?"

"I'll try, sir."

Between that game and the next one with the Wildcats, Chris kept reminding himself of what Mr. Snedecker had said. He made up his mind to loosen up, relax, not worry, believe in himself, have confidence.

Everything was fine, until he stepped on the field. Then there was the same dryness in his mouth, the same stiffness in his joints and muscles, the same helpless trembling inside. There was the confusion of instructions in his head, the paralyzing indecision when anything unexpected happened. But this time the confusion was worse than ever because added to all the old instructions were the new ones about loosening up, not worrying, and having confidence.

The Bears won, four to two, to keep their first-place position. But Chris, who escaped striking out three times only because once a pitched ball brushed his leg to put him on base, did nothing to help.

Watching Hobie play for the opposing team made Chris feel even more worthless. Hobie smashed out three singles, stole two bases, and performed flawlessly behind the plate. For such a tiny boy, it was an amazing performance. Chris tried to imagine how good Hobie would be if he were as big as himself.

More than ever, Chris realized how lucky he was that Hobie was his friend. For by this time they had become inseparable. Chris waked in the morning to the ringing of the telephone, which was always Hobie with some plan for their day.

Chris and Hobie went swimming. They played miniature golf. They bowled. They roller-skated. They competed in shooting baskets at the outdoor court in the park. Hobie was good at everything.

Often they went to Hobie's house. It was the sort of house where a boy could feel at home—old and roomy and comfortably shabby. In the basement were a pool table, a pingpong table, and an elaborate model railroad setup. In the kitchen was a refrigerator always filled with food and cold drinks. In Hobie's bedroom were a television set, a radio, and a record player with lots of records. The walls were lined with shelves of trophies inscribed to "H. Timmons" for excellence in every sport from archery to water skiing. In the attic was Hobie's model shop, crowded with miniature cars, ships and airplanes. In the back yard was a disused barn where Hobie kept a set of weights, boxing gloves and a punching bag, four bicycles of various sizes and ages, several sleeping bags, and a tent.

Sharing all this abundance with Hobie were only a small, quiet, gray-haired couple. Chris at first supposed these were Hobie's grandparents. Then, to his surprise, he discovered that they were his parents.

Chris always had fun with Hobie, no matter what they did. But he enjoyed most the days at Hobie's house. In the first place, there were more different things to do there than anywhere else. In the second place, there was never any trouble there. And, away from Hobie's house there seemed to be constant trouble.

There was the time he and Hobie were at the pool practicing underwater swimming, and a pretty red-haired girl had accused Chris of knocking her feet out from under her. And the time at the skating rink, when someone had dropped a very real-looking rubber snake onto the track. And the time when several customers had stormed out of the snack bar at the bowling alley vowing never to return, and it had then been discovered that someone had filled the sugar dispenser with salt. Chris had been blamed for every one of those things. In fact, he was beginning to think that everybody in Millbrook was just waiting for something to go wrong so they could blame him for it. And nobody except Hobie would ever believe his denials.

All in all, it was a most confusing summer. Was he a home-run hero or a bungler? Was he a juvenile delinquent or an ordinarily well-behaved twelve-year-old? Chris reached the point where he just didn't know what he was. He felt as if there were only one sure thing in the world. That was the friendship of the greatest kid he'd ever met, Hobie Timmons.

CHAPTER 13

A Crash Like Thunder

THE FIRST OF JULY started like all the other recent days. First the insistent ringing of the telephone, then his mother's voice calling Chris's name.

Chris staggered sleepily down the hall and picked up the receiver. He tried to sound alert, but Hobie wasn't fooled.

"Boy! If it wasn't for me you'd waste your whole life sleeping. What you doing today?"

"Nothing. What would you like to do?"

"I thought we might mess around down town. Want to meet me on the corner?"

"No, you don't!" Chris's mother set down the pitcher of orange juice with a thump. "You tell Hobie he can come in and wait while you eat your breakfast."

Hobie's high-pitched giggle came over the wire, then his shrill voice. "Tell your mother I'll be right there," and the receiver, clicked down.

"You embarrassed me, Mom," Chris grumbled when he returned dressed and washed and combed. "Hobie was talking to me, not you."

Mrs. Sorensen laughed. "If Hobie doesn't want me to hear, he should keep his voice down. He doesn't even need a telephone." She set down a plate filled with scrambled eggs and bacon, and beside it a smaller one heaped with buttered toast. "Now, take your time and eat a good breakfast. You and Hobie have all day to enjoy yourselves. Come to think of it, it won't hurt Hobie to relax a few minutes while he's waiting. He's such a sweet boy. But sometimes he scares me."

"Scares you? Why?" Chris waited with his fork in mid-air for his mother to answer. But before she could, there was a light, swift tapping at the door.

"Come in, Hobie," Chris's mother called.

There was nothing relaxed about the way Hobie sat while he waited. He perched on the edge of his seat, skinny legs twined about the chair legs, elbows jammed down hard on the table, tiny hands clasped together so tight the knuckles were white.

"Have something to eat while you're waiting,

Hobie," Mrs. Sorensen coaxed. "How about an egg and some toast?"

Hobie's blue eyes beamed appreciation, and he smiled radiantly. "Thank you very much, ma'am, but I couldn't. I've already had breakfast."

"Not even a glass of juice?"

"Well—if you're sure it's not too much trouble."

"Not a bit." Chris's mother poured a brimming glass and set it in front of Hobie.

He sipped it, and a look of pleased surprise swept over his face. "This is delicious orange juice, Mrs. Sorensen. Best I've ever tasted."

"But it was just regular orange juice. You didn't even like it enough to drink it all," Chris complained when they were outside.

"I know." Hobie grinned smugly. "But women like to be told things are the best you ever tasted. So why not? Doesn't cost anything."

"But if it's not true?" Chris protested.

Hobie shrugged. "What's the difference? If you go to a party, you always say you had a good time. Even if you could just barely live through it."

"Mm—I guess so." To Chris it still seemed deceitful. But he'd learned not to argue with Hobie. Hobie was always two steps ahead of him, and whenever Chris disagreed with him he ended up feeling like a candidate for a stupidity award.

With anybody else, walking around Millbrook might have been boring. With Hobie, it was an adventure. They started at the Super-Value Used Car lot, where Hobie examined and criticized the merchandise on display.

Finally, in a remote corner of the lot, he stopped in front of a battered vehicle with a crumpled fender, a cracked windshield, and a general air of impending collapse. "That's my baby!" he announced. "I've almost got my parents talked into buying it."

"For you? But it'll be years before you're old enough for a license," Chris objected. "Besides, what do you want with a wreck like that?"

"You wait! Time I get through, I'll have a hotrod to make people's eyes pop. Put it back in the barn, strip it down, rebuild it from the wheels up. You can help," he assured Chris generously.

From there they went to the hobby shop, where Hobie ordered a couple of new accessories for his model railroad. Then they spent some time watching a new sidewalk under construction. They departed hastily after a big dog which had been ambling by suddenly raced across the soft cement, leaving a trail of crater-like footprints.

"You big clown!" one of the workmen roared, as Chris followed Hobie around the nearest corner. Once more he was being blamed for something he'd had nothing to do with.

When it seemed safe to stop, they were in front of Millbrook's largest supermarket. "Hey!" Hobie cried. "Let's buy some grub. We can eat over in the park. Then we won't have to go home."

"I didn't bring any money," Chris objected.

"That's all right. I've got some." Hobie darted inside, and Chris followed.

The place was crowded with women pushing carts, and with small children. There were long lines at the checkout counters. For a moment Chris couldn't find Hobie. Then he saw him, standing beside a tall pyramid of cans topped by a sign, BAR-GAIN SPECIAL—TOMATOES, 4 CANS $1.00. Chris joined him. "What'll we buy?" he asked.

"Let's start with some pretzels. Then we'll see what else looks good."

Chris never knew what made him drop his eyes at that moment. But drop them he did, and what he saw made a shock like a bolt of electricity go all through him. It was a small foot in a grimy sneaker, and it was hooking itself behind one of the cans in the foundation of the pyramid.

There was a crash like thunder, an erratic series of thuds, and a chorus of panicky screams. The pyramid had collapsed, and cans of tomatoes were rolling in all directions. They banged into shelves, and crashed into walls. They entangled themselves with the wheels of carts and with the feet of terrified shoppers.

When the manager came rushing up, Chris was standing there, red-faced and guilty-looking. Hobie was two aisles away, innocently examining the shelves of pretzels and potato chips.

The manager scolded, threatened to call the police, then relented on condition that Chris replace the scattered cans and promise never to enter his store again.

Chris stood silent through it all, then said, "I'm sorry, sir," and began the job of repairing the damage.

It was only then that Hobie appeared, looking shocked and sympathetic. "It was an accident, sir," he told the manager earnestly. "It must have been. I'll help clean up."

The manager smiled down at Hobie and said, "Thank you, son." Then he glared at Chris and growled, "You're lucky to have a friend that'll stick by you. Most kids would be a couple of blocks away by this time."

At last every can was retrieved, and placed in a low, solid stack. Chris was sure half the women in town had seen his humiliation. Soon everyone would know about it. But at least he was free to leave, and escape from the indignant glares.

"Let's go over to my house," Hobie piped, when they were outside.

Chris shook his head and walked away.

"What's the matter?" Hobie called after him, "What did I do?"

Chris walked faster. But he could still hear Hobie yelling, "All right, you big sorehead. See if I care!"

The one sure thing in the world had vanished as if it had never been. And, Chris realized bitterly, it *had* never been. Hobie had never really been his friend. He'd only been using him, all along, to take the blame for his shabby, childish little tricks. How in the world had he been stupid enough to go along all this time without seeing that?

The worst thing was that there was nothing he could do. He couldn't fight Hobie, because Hobie was too small. He couldn't tell anybody. Whoever heard would take him for a liar. Or, worse yet, for a fool.

The only thing to do was to keep quiet and stay away from Hobie. Chris wished he might never have to lay eyes on Hobie again as long as he lived.

[CHAPTER 14]

Chris--Spelled with a K

NEXT MORNING Hobie called as usual. Chris hoped it was to say he was sorry, but there was no trace of regret in Hobie's voice. So he said curtly, "I'm busy," and hung up. Hobie didn't call again.

After the period of constant, exciting activity, Chris's life was suddenly emptier than ever. Once more the Sorensens' yard became a place of manicured perfection. Once more the garage and cellar were spic and span. Once more Chris's mother began to give him puzzled and anxious looks. But she asked no questions.

It was Chris who asked questions, of himself. Or, rather, just one question. Why? Why had Hobie treated him that way? For of course he'd been treating him the same, from that first evening when his candy-throwing had caused Chris to be ejected from the theater.

It was easy now to see that Hobie had pretended to make friends just to cause Chris trouble. It was obvious that all along Hobie had been inwardly laughing at the stupid, gullible fool who let himself be made the goat for Hobie's misbehavior. It was easy enough to say that Hobie was a rotten, sneaky, hateful little rat.

But, why? What did Hobie gain by acting that way? Remembering what Kayo had told him, remembering things other boys had said and the way they'd looked when they saw him with Hobie, Chris knew he wasn't the first Hobie had treated in this way. He'd driven away other friends. But why?

Only a stupid kid would keep doing the things Hobie did. But Hobie wasn't stupid. Anybody who talked to him for five minutes would know that. So, why? Why, if Hobie wasn't stupid, did he keep doing stupid things?

To make life even duller, there came a spell of rainy weather. For a full week there wasn't even a Little League game to vary Chris's monotonous routine.

At last there were two clear days in a row. The postponed game with the Colts was scheduled for

Saturday afternoon. Chris concentrated on feeling confident. But the more fiercely he ordered himself to relax, the stiffer he became. He even tried telling himself it didn't matter how he played, since the Colts were such a feeble team. That didn't help, either. He knew this game would be like all the rest.

But he soon learned that in one way it would be very different. As Tommy stepped to the plate to lead off, a piercing voice cried, "No batter up there, kid! First strikeout comin' up!"

It was Hobie, just behind the wire-mesh fence on the first base side. Chris had to look twice before he could believe his eyes. For Hobie never came to Little League games. He had hooted scornfully when Chris had once suggested they go watch the Tigers play the Stags. "Fat chance!" Hobie had scoffed. "Baseball's all right if you're playing. But who wants to sit around and watch a bunch of other guys play?" Still, here he was.

At all the games, there was a good deal of noise from the crowd. Cheers, groans, bits of advice, laughter. But Chris couldn't remember any spectator as loudly or as constantly vocal as Hobie. He heckled the Bears with sarcastic remarks and derisive laughter. To the Colts he yelled encouragement and shrewd if sometimes unsportsmanlike advice. And it began to seem that Hobie was backing a winner.

Though Pat was pitching well, the Colts scored in the first inning when a batter walked, advanced on Mark's error and a fielder's choice, and scored on a sacrifice bunt.

The Colts' pitcher was a stocky boy with horn-rimmed glasses, who threw a ball anyone could hit. Practically everybody but Chris, who struck out twice, did hit it with ease. The Bears racked up numerous hits, and twice even loaded the bases. But, somehow, nobody could score. When the Bears prepared for their last chance in the top of the sixth, they trailed by one to nothing.

Pat, the first batter, drove the first pitch into short left for a single. Mark followed with a bouncer to the shortstop that forced Pat at second. Then came Kayo. He took a called strike, a ball, then drove a single up the middle. Mark was off fast, tore around second without slowing down, and slid safely into third.

Men on first and third, only one out. Jerry was the batter. "He's gonna steal!" Hobie shrilled. "Let him go—what do you care?"

Whether because of Hobie's advice or not, there

was no throw when Jerry took a called strike and Kayo headed for second. Instead of scoring the hoped-for run, Mark had to dive back to third. Jerry popped up the next pitch, and the Colts' catcher took it for the second out.

Sandy was blowing one of his more perfect bubbles as he strolled to the plate. He paused to let it burst before he took his usual crouching stance. As he waited for the pitch, he looked as carelessly at ease as if the Bears had enjoyed a ten-run lead.

Chris put on a helmet and picked up a couple of bats. He'd be next, unless Sandy made the final out.

"No batter!" Hobie screamed joyfully. "This fat little clown can't hit."

Sandy's grin widened as he took a pitch outside. Next time he swung and hit a slow bouncer toward third. The third baseman came in to grab it, but Sandy was too close to first for a throw, and the bases were loaded.

The air was heavy with suspense as Chris headed for the plate. The crowd was tense with excitement, waiting to see what he would do. Anything, even a base on balls, would score a run and keep the Bears' hopes alive. But Chris knew the crowd expected much more than that.

"Come on, you big Swede!" "Now's the time—hit one out of here!" "You can do it, Chris!" the excited voices clamored.

Everyone seemed excited but Chris himself. He could feel nothing but dull, numb despair. This pitcher wasn't passing out walks, and he'd already struck him out twice today.

Then he heard Hobie's piercing voice. "Big Swede? Huh! Big Whiff, you mean! Name's Chris—spelled with a *K*."

The anger that boiled up inside Chris left no room for any other feeling. Why, the little rat! "Chris spelled with a *K*—" All through the stands people were laughing. If they didn't already know that *K* stood for strikeout in the score book, someone sitting near-by was ready to tell them. Leave it to Hobie to think of a thing like that! The pitch was coming in, and suddenly the ball seemed to have Hobie's grinning face.

It was asking to be smashed, and smash it he did. There was a heavier, duller feeling as he hit it. And, as he ran, he saw that the ball was going too high, arching and falling instead of soaring as it usually did when he hit it. But, as it fell, it barely cleared the fence. It scored four runs, and in the bottom of the inning Pat set down the shaken Colts in order. The Bears had another victory, four to one.

Chris wasn't surprised when his teammates swarmed around to pound him on the back and shout congratulations. A last-inning grand slam was enough to get anybody excited. He was surprised that Mr. Snedecker seemed beside himself with joy. When the others had gone, he told him why.

"My goodness, boy! You hit a bad pitch that time. Not that I recommend swinging at bad pitches, but—you see, when you hit those other home runs it was because the pitcher laid it right in that groove where you always swing. This time he didn't put it in there for you. You went after it. That's what I've been waiting for. Now you've got the feel of it."

Chris nodded and mumbled his thanks. No use telling Mr. Snedecker it had only happened because he'd been so angry at Hobie. When he could get away, he walked up toward the parking lot. His father would be waiting.

A group of Colts' players was walking some distance ahead. As Chris watched, Hobie ran up to join them. "Tough luck, fellows," Hobie said, "I hoped you'd win." The Colts looked at Hobie coldly, said nothing, and walked a little faster.

Chris walked slowly so as not to catch up with

Hobie. He hoped Hobie wouldn't notice him. Not far ahead was the ice cream truck with the usual line of customers. Moving slowly past were the groups of those who would have liked to be customers but couldn't afford to be. Among these were some of Hobie's teammates on the Wildcats.

Hobie ran up to them, and Chris heard him call, "Hey, you guys! How about an ice cream? My treat."

There was a unanimous shaking of heads. Someone said, "No you don't, Timmons!" Someone else said, "Get lost, you little rat."

With a laugh and a shrug of his narrow shoulders, Hobie turned away. The movement brought him face to face with Chris, but it was plain he wasn't aware of him, or of anyone watching. For a revealing moment, Hobie's was the saddest, the most desperately lonely face Chris had ever seen.

In another instant Hobie had turned away. Chris knew that once more the habitual grin was on his face. But suddenly Chris realized that if anybody in the world needed a friend, it was Hobie. He needed a *real* friend—the kind he'd probably never had in all his life.

Chris broke into a run. He caught up with Hobie and dropped a hand on his shoulder. "Hi, there!"

he said. "How about us taking a bike ride tomorrow? We'll go out to Fiddler's Lake."

"Huh? Oh—well—" Hobie was struggling with amazement, maybe even with suspicion. "Nobody goes to Fiddler's Lake. Nothing to do there."

But Chris insisted. "It's a nice ride. We'll take our lunch. What do you say?"

For a moment Hobie hesitated. Then he said, "Well—sure! What time should we start?"

CHAPTER 15

Like a Big Man

FIDDLER'S LAKE WAS SIX MILES from Millbrook. The boys took the least traveled of the roads out of town, turned onto another that was narrow and dusty, then bumped along a rutted lane that seemed not to have been used for years. Hobie had been right. Nobody went to Fiddler's Lake. When they arrived, it was easy to see why.

The muddy patch of water might more justly have been called a pond. A few scrawny trees grew beside it. The strip of barren earth on one side that might have been called a beach was littered with jagged stones.

"See?" Hobie demanded. "Nothing to do. Too small for boats. Not deep enough to swim. Never even heard of anybody catching a fish. Why'd you want to come here, anyway?"

"That's why," Chris replied. "I'm tired of rushing around with a lot of people. Out here you can have some peace and quiet. And privacy."

"Privacy for what?" Hobie demanded, stepping back a couple of paces. "I know! You got me out here just to get even—"

"Get even for what?" Chris inquired innocently. "You never did anything I'd want to get even for—did you, Hobie?"

Hobie laughed nervously. "Well—of course not! Only I thought you might have some idea—you know!"

Chris shook his head. "I thought we were friends. You don't expect a friend to play a dirty trick on you."

"Okay—forget it!" Hobie said plaintively. "I didn't mean anything. Can't a fellow open his mouth without your making a federal case out of it?"

They wandered around a while, idly exploring. That is, Chris did. Hobie ran ahead, doubled back, dashed off to one side or the other, keeping up a continual chatter. He reminded Chris of a nervous, yapping little terrier.

Chris began to get bored, but he didn't regret coming. Having nobody around meant Hobie couldn't get him into trouble if he tried. Having nothing to do meant that perhaps just for lack of anything better Hobie would say or do something to help Chris answer the question that had been baffling him. Why did such a bright kid persist in doing such stupid things? So far Hobie had revealed nothing except that he seemed unable to do nothing, even when there was nothing to do.

They completed their circuit of the pond. Chris flopped down on the wiry grass under a tree and closed his eyes. But Hobie was not content to do the same.

"I knew how it would be," he complained. "Nothing to do. So I brought along something. Look here, Chris."

"Why don't you take it easy, Hobie?" Chris grumbled. But Hobie wouldn't, so at last Chris got reluctantly to his feet. Hobie was standing beside his bicycle, undoing the straps on the saddlebag. He took out two spray-cans of paint.

Chris frowned. "What are those for?"

"To paint our bikes," Hobie explained, handing one to Chris. "Neat idea, huh, painting our bikes to match? I just happened to think of it, so I picked these up at the Hobby Shop."

"Sounds all right," Chris agreed, "but—"

Hobie waited a moment. "But what?"

"Nothing," Chris said innocently. "It's a great idea."

They set up the bikes near the water's edge. Hobie fussed around, moving his several times, examining and shaking up his can of paint. At last he burst out impatiently, "Aw, we can't paint these things here. If we want to do a decent job, we'll have to take 'em apart, clean 'em up, and all that. We'd better do it over at my place, in the barn."

"That's right," Chris agreed.

"Suppose these two cans really match?" Hobie wondered after a moment. "Sometimes they don't, even when they're marked the same. Let's try 'em out."

"All right," Chris said.

They opened the cans, sprayed some of the larger rocks, and waited for the paint to dry. Hobie nodded with satisfaction. "They're all right. You keep one, and bring it over tomorrow."

"All right." Chris stowed the can in his saddle-bag.

The bright green rocks struck a jarring note on the beach, so Chris and Hobie got them out of sight by throwing them in the lake. That led to a competition in pebble-skipping, and then to a rock-throwing contest. Hobie won, by a narrow margin,

for accuracy. For distance, Chris was so far ahead
that Hobie gave up in disgust.

"It's not fair though, with me so much bigger,"
Chris said comfortingly.

"You hear me complaining?" Hobie snarled.

"No—of course not," Chris admitted hastily.

The sun was low in the sky when the boys headed
back toward Millbrook. The longer they had stayed
at Fiddler's Lake the more things they had found
to do and talk about. Still, Chris felt no nearer to
understanding Hobie than he had in the beginning.

The way back seemed longer than the way out.
By the time they reached Millbrook and entered a
broad street lined with the town's most impressive
houses, darkness had fallen.

About that time, Hobie began to lag behind. At
once Chris came alert. He had a pretty good idea
what Hobie intended to do. But he was determined
that though things might start as usual they would
end differently. This time he had no intention of
being Hobie's scapegoat.

Chris had kept up a leisurely but steady speed
all the way. Now he turned into a driveway and
stood silent in the shadow of some tall shrubbery.
Moments later Hobie appeared. He stopped, so
close Chris could almost have reached out and

touched him. Then he proceeded to spray a complicated, whirling design in green paint on the mailbox that stood at the end of the drive. When he started down the street again Chris followed, feeling like a detective shadowing a suspect.

There wasn't much traffic. The few cars that had passed hadn't even slowed up. But suddenly Chris heard the sound of a quick stop, a pause, a hurried start. Looking back, he saw a police car.

Chris sped ahead. Just as the car caught up with him, he caught up with Hobie. Just as a tall young policeman jumped out of the car and grabbed Chris's arm, Chris grabbed Hobie's.

"What's the idea?" the policeman demanded. "Doing a crazy thing like that? Now I'll have to take you to the station. We'll have to call your parents, and that won't make them happy. You'll have to go to court. Now, you tell me—was it worth it?"

"But I didn't do it, sir," Chris said very politely.

"Didn't *do* it! Don't give me that. I spotted one of your paint jobs and stopped the car. When I started up, the first thing I saw was you, trying for a getaway. And—let me see that saddlebag." Chris opened it. There was the can of paint. The policeman examined it. "Same color, and it's been used. But I'd still like to know why."

"Sir—" Chris searched desperately for the right thing to say. He couldn't squeal on Hobie. And the policeman still hadn't seen him—or, if he had, he took him for an innocent, tag-along little brother. But—the policeman was very tall. Perhaps, without really being told, he could understand.

"Please don't get mad," Chris said, "but why do you think kids usually do things like this?"

"I suppose it makes them feel important," the tall man said slowly. "A kid gets away with this kind of stupid trick, he tells his friends, figures he looks like a big man."

"Well, sir—do you think somebody my size really needs that?" Chris almost held his breath as he waited for the policeman's reply.

He watched a thoughtful frown come over the tall man's face and then felt the grip on his arm loosen. At last the policeman spoke. "You, there!" he ordered. "Come out here where I can see you."

For a moment he looked speculatively down at Hobie, while Hobie glared defiantly back. Then, "Let's see what's in your saddlebag," he said.

"You don't have to look," Hobie shrilled, "I did it. And it's not so I could look big, either. I just—I just felt like it."

CHAPTER 16

A Friend in Need

"LET'S GO, CHRIS!" Mr. Sorensen called. It was Saturday, the day after the trip to Fiddler's Lake. The Bears were playing the Lions in the first game of a doubleheader. This time all the Sorensens would be there. They were ready and waiting.

Chris picked up his glove, put on his cap, and plodded gloomily toward the car. His mother was in the back seat, and beside her his little sisters bounced and squealed with anticipation. Though they didn't understand baseball, they knew their brother was a hero, and were expecting to see him do something splendid.

What a hope! In spite of what Mr. Snedecker had said after the last game, Chris knew that nothing was changed. There was no more chance than there had ever been that he would manage to become a real hitter. That home run, which by sheer chance had happened to be a grand slam and to win the game, had been just as fluky as all the rest. He'd swung outside his usual groove only because he'd been blind with rage at Hobie.

Today Chris hardly cared whether he played or not. He was too worried about Hobie. The minute Hobie had admitted his guilt, the policeman had ordered Chris to go home, and Chris had gone.

Before he'd gone a block, Chris's conscience had begun to torment him. It hadn't stopped since except for the few hours he'd slept. He kept seeing Hobie at the station house, surrounded by police. The more he thought about it, the more pathetically small Hobie seemed to become.

Then he imagined Hobie's gentle, gray-haired parents, and how shocked and sorry they must be. Chris almost wished he'd never caught up with Hobie—that he'd taken the blame on his own broad shoulders instead of dropping it on Hobie's slender ones. Almost he wished that, but not quite.

Even as Chris tried to eat the dinner his mother had kept warm for him, he expected the phone to ring and to hear Hobie tell him what had happened. Afterward he only half listened to his mother's lecture about the dangers of bicycle riding on dark streets and the importance of getting home on time. Even when he was in bed he couldn't stop listening for the telephone.

But it didn't ring—neither that night nor the next morning. A couple of times Chris picked up the receiver and started to dial Hobie's number. But each time he stopped and hung up. Hobie must be too angry to want to talk to him, or he would have called. A prospect even worse than Hobie's anger was the thought that one of Hobie's parents might answer, and accuse him of leading their son into trouble. For who would ever believe it hadn't been the big one of the two who'd been the leader?

The first thing Chris heard when he joined the team was Mark's delighted announcement that Hobie had at last gotten himself in real trouble. Rejoicing was unanimous.

"Best news I've heard all summer," Kayo chortled. "See, Chris? Didn't I tell you that little pipsqueak was no good?"

"About time!" Sandy gloated. "Remember when I got kept in for a week, when Hobie threw a rock through Mrs. McBride's picture window and I got blamed?"

"Yeah!" Tommy agreed, "People always thought

he was such a little angel. The little rat! What'll they do? Send him to reform school, I hope?"

"Don't know," Mark said. "First he's got to clean up a bunch of stuff he painted last night. That'll keep him busy for a while."

Chris said nothing. He didn't feel like joining the celebration over Hobie's downfall. Neither did he feel like defending Hobie. Remembering the trouble Hobie had caused him, he couldn't blame the others for feeling as they did. He felt confused and distracted, as if he were only half there.

When the game started, that was the way he played. It wasn't only that he could do no better at bat than a walk and two strikeouts. Nothing unusual about that. But when he muffed two easy chances at first and blotted his record with two errors, his misery became total.

The game was a real disaster. Sandy's pitching wasn't up to par, and when Kayo relieved in the third, he provided little improvement. The Bears' hitting wasn't up to par, either. The lack-luster contest dragged out its six innings, and ended in a seven to two victory for the Lions.

Even if Chris hadn't had anywhere to go after the game, he'd have been eager to escape from the house as soon as he'd changed his clothes. His family was feeling sorry for him, trying to find something nice to say when there wasn't anything. Chris got on his bike and headed for the spot where he'd left Hobie the night before.

Long before he reached it, Chris noticed an unusual amount of traffic on the quiet street. There were boys walking, alone or in groups. There were boys on bicycles. Then he came upon a real crowd.

Chris parked his bike and eased his way through a semicircle of boys. As he'd guessed, Hobie was its center. Tight-lipped and silent, he was scraping spatters of green paint from a mailbox.

"Three down and five to go," somebody remarked. "Another day or two."

"I just inspected that last one," someone else giggled. "You missed a couple of spots."

"How's the arm feeling, Hobie?" another voice taunted. "Don't worry—I'll bring you a bottle of liniment."

A dark-haired boy Chris didn't know was drinking a bottle of soda. "Hey, Hobe!" he called. "You look thirsty. Have a drink." Shaking up the bottle, he aimed a spray that struck Hobie's cheek. Hobie winced but said nothing and went on scraping.

Suddenly Chris had had enough. Turning to face

the jeering crowd, he said loudly, "Okay, you guys. You can all go home now."

"How come?"

"What's the idea?"

"Who put you in charge?"

"Who's going to make us?"

Chris answered the protests calmly and in turn. "Because you shouldn't pick on a guy when he's down. Hobie's got to clean up this mess, but there's no reason why he's got to take your razzing. Who put me in charge? Me! And anybody that thinks I can't make him get out of here can stick around and see what happens."

There was some grumbling, but in about two minutes everybody had gone. Chris sighed with relief. For once, he was glad to be so big. He didn't like to fight, and wasn't good at it. If his size hadn't made everybody afraid to take up his challenge, he'd have been sunk.

He turned back toward Hobie. "I'll give you a hand." He picked up a piece of steel wool and started scouring.

"Trying to make up for squealing on me, huh?" Hobie demanded.

"I didn't squeal on you," Chris said. "I made

you squeal on yourself. Would you rather I just steered clear of you, like everybody else?"

For a long time the two scraped and scrubbed in silence. At last Hobie spoke, in a voice unexpectedly soft and uncertain. "You did right, Chris. That policeman last night—Officer Bradley, his name is—talked to me a long time after you left. He made me see that when I was trying hardest to act big, I was really being—well, even smaller than I am. And, you know what? He didn't take me to the station at all. Didn't even call my parents. Said he'd let me tell them myself, any way I wanted to. And he said he'd guarantee if I cleaned up the mess, none of the people would complain."

"That's great," Chris said. "So now why don't you just forget about being big or small and act natural— like yourself? You might turn out to be a pretty good kid and surprise everybody."

Hobie giggled. "They'd never believe it. But I think I might give it a try."

CHAPTER 17

All-Star Material

NEXT MORNING CHRIS WOKE to the early ringing of the telephone, and the comfortable knowledge that he and Hobie were friends again. He wondered what new excitements Hobie was planning for the day.

But this call wasn't Hobie's usual demand that Chris meet him right after church and rush off somewhere. He started on a different subject entirely. "Hey, Chris! Did you make the all-stars?"

Chris scowled at the receiver for a moment, wondering how even Hobie could be so tactless. He knew there was no hope that a fumbler like himself, who never did anything good except by the sheerest luck, could make the Millbrook All-Stars. So why did Hobie have to bring up the subject?

"Of course not!" he said. "Who did make it besides you, Hobe?"

"I only know for sure about the ones from the Wildcats," Hobie replied. "There's me and our best pitcher, Coleman. Then there's Pete Roberts, our first baseman. But I could guess a few others. I'd say, from your team Kayo and Mark. And you. Aren't you kidding me, Chris? I thought sure you'd make it."

"No," Chris said. He wished Hobie would stop this, and talk about something else.

"Oh, well—" Hobie was silent for a moment. Then he said brightly, "See you after church, then. Meet you on the corner?"

"All right."

Chris went to get washed up and dressed. By the odors from the kitchen he could tell breakfast was almost ready. His vigorous splashing drowned out the ringing of the telephone, and his mother had to bang on the bathroom door before he realized someone was calling him. He wondered what Hobie could have forgotten that would be important enough to make him call back.

But it wasn't Hobie's voice. It was Mr. Snedecker's. "Morning, Chris," it said cheerfully. "Hope I didn't wake you up."

"No, I was awake," Chris assured him.

"Just wanted to make sure you'd be at all-star practice tomorrow. Five o'clock."

Chris nearly choked with astonishment. He got out some sounds that made no sense, and heard Mr. Snedecker chuckle. "Why, Chris! You didn't think we'd forget our home-run champ, did you? See you tomorrow, and we'll start getting the team in shape."

His mother and father were delighted at the news, but neither seemed surprised. Maybe, Chris thought, he should have expected it. Hobie had. And seemingly Mr. Snedecker had taken it for granted. If they all thought he deserved it—well, perhaps he did.

When Chris told Hobie what had happened, Hobie nodded smugly. "I told you," he said. "I checked and found out everybody who's on the team, and just listen to this! Weeks ago I wrote down a list of the kids I thought they'd pick, and I only missed one. Pretty good, huh?"

"Sure is," Chris said admiringly. "You never worried at all that you might not make it?"

Hobie laughed. "Me—worry? Why should I? I've got the highest batting average in the league.

Plus that, I've caught twelve whole games with only one error. How could they keep me off?"

Chris couldn't help feeling a twinge of envy as he compared Hobie's record with his own. "Guess there's no reason you should have worried," he admitted. "But—how do you figure they think I can fit in? I've never even dared to figure out my average, but it can't be much. Those three home runs were the only hits I had all season. And, errors—I had two just in our last game."

"That's easy," Hobie told him. "They won't figure you for starting lineup. Mr. Snedecker's too smart for that. He'll make sure everybody hears about those three home runs—two tape-measure jobs and a grand slam. He'll try to have you lose a few in batting practice, and make sure the other team sees. Then he'll keep you on the bench—maybe let the word get out you pulled a muscle in your leg or something so you can't play steady. That way the opposing pitcher can worry about when they might put you in to pinch-hit. That's known as psychological warfare, chum. Just wait and see if I'm not right."

Chris nodded. "You're right, Hobie. I can see that now, without waiting." The triumph he had felt when he heard Mr. Snedecker's words faded as Chris recognized the truth.

Hobie, Kayo, Mark, and all the others could rejoice in having earned a chance to test themselves against the best players from other towns. But he, Chris, would be with them only because he was so big and because he'd been so lucky.

He'd sit on the bench, like a scarecrow whose power to frighten depended on letting no one get close enough to see what he was really made of. Mr. Snedecker would never dare put him into a game and risk having everyone discover that his giant was only a dummy stuffed with straw.

CHAPTER 18

Forced Out at Second

THE FIRST TWO ALL-STAR PRACTICES reminded Chris of tryouts. Mr. Snedecker and his assistant, Mr. Roe of the Wildcats, put the boys through the same drill—running, fielding, throwing, batting. They watched with cool, critical eyes, exchanging muttered comments and making notes in little books.

"Anybody'd think we were strangers," Kayo complained, as they left the field after the second practice. "After practically a whole season, they ought to know what we can do."

"But you know the way they pick these teams," Pete Roberts said. "Mostly for hitting. I suppose if you were the best pitcher in the league they'd take you whether you could hit or not. But otherwise they wouldn't. So look what they've got. Six pitchers. Of course they can all play some other position, too. Four catchers, three first basemen, a shortstop and a flock of outfielders. And nobody that's ever played second or third. Mr. Snedecker and Mr. Roe have got to pull a team out of that grab-bag. You think that's easy?"

"Wow!" Mark cried in happy surprise. "Guess I got a break, being the only shortstop in the crowd."

Hobie, surprisingly, was silent until he and Chris had turned off on their separate way. Then he said with a grin, "Too bad those managers wouldn't ask me. They'd save themselves a lot of time. You watch the way this teams shapes up. Then see if I wasn't right." He handed Chris a folded piece of paper.

Chris nodded, and tucked the paper into his pocket. He was sure that when the team took shape and he read the names Hobie had written down, it would turn out that Hobie's prophesying average had been amazingly high. The longer Chris knew Hobie, the more convinced he became that there were few things the smaller boy couldn't do.

It even seemed that Hobie was beginning to overcome the dislike he had earned for himself among the boys of Millbrook. In the two all-star practices, he'd been a model of good behavior—

quiet, unassuming, helpful and polite. Already the looks of disbelief and suspicion that had greeted him on the first day had begun to fade. At this rate, Chris thought, it wouldn't be long until Hobie's name of Holy Terror would be forgotten.

Then came the third day of practice. "We've got a fine lot of ball players here," Mr. Snedecker told the assembled boys. "Now let's put a team together and have a little fielding practice. Nothing final about this lineup. But we'll see how it works. The rest of you—the ones I don't send out to positions—can take turns being baserunners."

The boys nodded, solemn-faced, rigid with suspense. Each was wishing for two things. First, to be chosen for the starting lineup. Second, to be assigned the position he regularly played, the one he knew he could fill best.

Only two of the fifteen weren't feeling that suspense, Chris thought. He wasn't, for he was resigned to being left out. Hobie wasn't. His blue eyes were gleaming with anticipation, and one small hand was already reaching toward the catcher's gear.

Then Mr. Snedecker began calling names. It made the occasion more solemn that he used full and correct names, instead of the nicknames most of the boys were used to.

"Charles Dawson, right field." A wiry boy in a Stags' uniform jumped up and ran into right field.

"Gerald Johnson, center field." As the Bears' catcher raced toward the outfield, Hobie threw Chris a wink and a smug grin.

"William Ryder, left field." Will was from the Tigers.

"Peter Roberts, first base." Chris winced inwardly, and realized that in spite of everything he'd still been hoping the place might be his.

"Hobart Timmons, second base."

Hobie's jaw dropped. He shook his head, in denial and disbelief. "But—but Mr. Snedecker, I'm a *catcher*," he protested.

Mr. Snedecker frowned. "Hobie," he said sternly, "on the Wildcats you were a catcher. Now you're a second baseman. Or you're nothing. Which will it be?"

Hobie's face reddened, then turned pale. For a moment he seemed undecided. Then he turned and walked slowly toward second base.

Chris hardly noticed as the rest of the players took their positions—Mark at shortstop, Bob Foster of the Colts at third, Kayo on the mound, husky Tom Scofield of the Lions catching.

The practice began. As it went on, Chris began

to be first angry with Hobie, then ashamed for him. While everyone else was trying to do his best, Hobie was trying to do his worst. He missed chance after chance, and when he did happen to get his hands on the ball, he made throws that were ridiculously bad.

To Chris's astonishment, Mr. Snedecker neither removed Hobie from the lineup nor said a single word of criticism or correction. With perfect calm and good humor, he simply ignored him.

※　　※　　※　　※　　※

"You were dogging it, Hobie. What were you trying to prove?" Chris demanded. They were the first words either he or Hobie had spoken, from the time they left the field after practice until they reached Hobie's house.

"That I'm not a second baseman," Hobie replied. "So, he'll have to let me catch."

"Suppose it doesn't work?"

"Then I won't stand for it. I'll quit!" Suddenly red-faced with fury, Hobie slammed down his glove on the floor of his front porch.

"Aw, Hobie—you don't mean that," Chris said coaxingly. "After all, you're in the starting lineup.

Suppose you were a benchwarmer like me? You'd have something to be mad about."

But Hobie wouldn't be soothed. His blue eyes still blazed with wrath as he flung his cap down beside the glove. "Just wait till people find out old Snedecker gave me such a bad time I had to quit the all-stars. He's going to hear some things he won't like!"

"But—Hobie, you'll be the one that's wrong if you quit. You ought to think about the good of the team, not just about where you want to play."

Hobie gave Chris a look of angry contempt. He kicked his glove and then his cap into the farthest corner of the porch. Then he said, "Let's go find something to eat. My folks went shopping. Guess they won't be back for a while."

For several minutes Chris and Hobie munched doughnuts and drank milk in silence. Then Hobie burst out again. "It's not fair! Chris, you know that lump Scofield's not half the catcher I am. He's so slow anybody would think he had anchors on his feet. You wait. He'll botch the job and Millbrook will lose their first game. Then everybody's going to say, 'If we had had Hobie in there we'd have won.' And who'll get blamed for my not being there? Ol' Know-It-All Snedecker, that's who!"

Chris shook his head. "Suppose you're right? Suppose everything turns out like you say? What good will it do? Will you be any better off sitting in the bleachers watching our team get beat than you would be trying to help us win? I just don't get it! What's so bad about playing second base?"

"Can't you understand *anything?*" Hobie demanded, in a voice almost inaudible with rage. "Can't you see Mr. Snedecker's *forcing* me out of the lineup? I *can't* play second—that's where the— that's where all the little *shrimps* play."

[CHAPTER 19]

Think Small!

AFTERWARD CHRIS WAS THANKFUL he'd been able to keep from laughing. For someone as angry as Hobie, to be able to laugh at himself would have been the best thing in the world. But to have someone else laugh at him would have been the worst. But Chris only figured that out later. At the time, it was pure instinct that told him he must hide his amusement behind a sympathetic face.

He even managed to say, after a moment, "You're right, Hobie. I don't blame you. Only—it's too bad for the team. Don't you care about the team at all?"

Chris could see Hobie's tension ease, the angry flush fade. "Sure—what do you think? Millbrook's my town. I've lived here all my life. But I told you. I can't play second base. Maybe there's some-

— 146 —

thing I can do to help the team, though. I think I know how to get you in the lineup."

"Me?" Chris shook his head. "But that's settled. I stay on the bench to scare the opposing team. If I ever go in to play—we're dead."

"Think so?" Hobie was himself again. He grinned, his eyes bright with excitement. "Come on. I got something to show you."

Hobie led the way to his room. He waved an arm at the shelves of trophies. "Take a good look at those," he said.

Chris groaned. For a moment he'd almost believed Hobie had something important—like a book that held the secret of athletic excellence. He said impatiently, "I've seen those, Hobie. I know you're good at any sport I could name and some I never heard of. And I know it stands to reason that if you're four-foot-six and weigh sixty pounds and can do all that, I should be able to do at least twice as much. I've told myself that a thousand times, but it never helped."

"I know that!" Hobie snapped. "Think I'm stupid? I mean, take a *good* look. The kind of look I never gave you a chance to take before."

Chris walked up to the shelves, and in a moment he saw what Hobie meant. Before, it had just been the large first letters of the names that stood out. Now that he could really see them, he realized that only a few really said "Hobie Timmons." The rest said "Henry Timmons," or "Howard Timmons," or "Harvey Timmons," or "Hubert Timmons." Some even said "Helen Timmons" or "Hope Timmons."

"But—but," Chris sputtered in bewilderment.

"Sure, I know," Hobie giggled. "You thought I was the only Timmons. A natural-born athletic genius whose doting parents gave him everything a kid's heart could desire. That's what I wanted you to think. I could put it over because you were new in town and didn't have friends to put you wise to the real picture. But now you know. Four brothers and two sisters. The youngest ten years older than me. All married and living far away. All big and handsome and athletic and popular. And all nice enough to leave me their trophies and all their other treasures—at least, until their own kids get old enough to appreciate them. How'd you like to be the runt of a litter like that?"

"Well—" Chris felt his face redden as he tried to think of something to say. "Guess that would be hard for anybody to live up to. But you've done all right."

Hobie nodded proudly. "But it didn't come natural. The way I did it's a secret I never thought I'd tell anybody. But you're my good buddy, so I'll let you in on it."

"A secret? What?" Chris demanded. It was ridiculous to imagine that a secret that would help little Hobie would also help him. Still, he was curious.

"Let's see," Hobie said thoughtfully. "I'll try to show it to you the way my father showed me. Come over to the window." Chris did. "Now put your hands up beside your eyes, so you can only see outside and not inside." Chris did. "Now how big a house are you in?"

"Well—uh—ten rooms or so. I never counted."

"But suppose you didn't know it was my house? Suppose somebody brought you in asleep, or blindfolded, or something? Could you tell then?" Hobie insisted.

"No. I'd have to look from the outside."

"So!" Hobie crowed triumphantly. "You're inside yourself, looking out. How can you tell how big you are, or how small? Only by looking from outside. Even if you look in a mirror you're looking from outside. Right?"

"Sure," Chris said.

"Well, then! As far as you know, you're as big as you think you are. As big as you want to be. My dad said, 'Think big, and you'll be big.' It took some getting used to, but it worked. Like, if I think I'm big enough to catch a line drive six inches out of my reach, I don't really get taller. But I can jump high enough to get it. See?"

"It's a great idea," Chris said admiringly, "but I don't see how it can help me."

"Just change it to fit you," Hobie explained. "Instead of thinking big, you think small. Think you're the size of—oh, Mark for instance."

"You really believe that would help?"

"I know it will," Hobie said. "I knew it that day at the lake. Remember? When we were throwing rocks, and you were putting them out of sight? Because we were all alone, nobody watching, and you forgot what size you were. But on the field, you can hardly get the ball from first to third. Everybody thinks you've got a weak arm—even you think so. But it's only because you think everybody's looking at you because you're so big. You tighten up, and sure enough you *can't* throw. But if you think yourself as small as you want to be, you won't worry about people looking at you. You'll throw the ball like you threw those rocks. And you'll swing a bat loose, the same way."

"Hey!" Chris cried in sudden excitement, "That's

what my father, and Mr. Snedecker, and—and everybody's been telling me. To relax, take it easy, loosen up. But none of them told me how. The more I tried, the more I tightened up. You're the first one that told me how. Now I can give it a real try. And you've got to help."

"Sure I'll help," Hobie assured him. "It's hard at first, but it gets easier. The important thing is to keep looking out, at everything but yourself. I'll bet you'll be able to tell the difference by the time we go to practice tomorrow. I—I mean, by the time *you* go to practice tomorrow."

"Hobie—please don't get mad. Just listen a minute," Chris said earnestly. "You told me an important secret, and I hope I can use it. But you're not using it yourself. Remember what Officer Bradley told you—that when you try too hard to be big you can make yourself smaller than you were to start with? You were smart enough to know he was right, and change. But now—don't you see you'll be doing the very same thing if you quit the all-stars?"

Hobie frowned. "How do you figure that?"

"You made yourself big enough to handle a big man's job—catching for the Wildcats. That was great. But would it be so important to you to hold down a big man's job if you really believed you were big? Wouldn't a *really* big man take on any job that needed doing? I'll bet it would never enter his head that any job could make him look small. You know, Mr. Snedecker's paying you a big compliment when he expects you to switch from catching to playing second. Are you going to give up and admit you're afraid to even try it?"

"I don't care what anybody thinks," Hobie declared sullenly. But there was uncertainty in his voice.

Chris knew he had to use the final appeal, the one he hated to use because it didn't seem quite fair. "Hobie—I'll never make this thing work well enough to get in the lineup if you don't stick around and help."

"Aw—how helpless can you get? All right, I'll string along. Anything for a pal." Hobie made a martyr's face, but Chris wasn't fooled. He knew that, though he'd never admit it, Hobie was as happy as himself at the way things had turned out.

CHAPTER 20

No Magic Today

WHEN CHRIS TRIED HOBIE'S FORMULA, he found it wasn't as easy as rubbing a lamp, putting on an enchanted ring, or mumbling an incantation. It took concentration, and mostly it didn't work.

But there were times when, suddenly, it did. Then there was no more paralyzing indecision about what to do next. His reactions became instinctively right, and his muscles obeyed them effortlessly.

Mr. Snedecker didn't notice the difference right away, but by the third practice he was watching Chris with puzzlement and delight. When he dismissed the boys, he asked Chris and Hobie to stay.

"Well, Chris!" he crowed, when they were alone, "I see you finally took my advice. See what you can do when you loosen up and play your game?"

"Yes, sir." Chris glanced at Hobie and saw that Hobie was sharing his secret amusement. Let Mr. Snedecker take credit for the change. He and Hobie knew who really deserved it.

"Keep up the good work and—my goodness, boy! There's no telling what you can do," Mr. Snedecker went on. "And—Hobie, second's not such a bad spot, is it?"

"Not too bad, sir," Hobie agreed.

"You're still hankering after that catcher's job. I can tell. But—my goodness, boy! All that speed of yours was wasted behind the plate. You're a born second baseman, and you'll be a real crackerjack when you stop getting distracted with wishing you were back in the catcher's box."

"I'll watch that, sir," Hobie said meekly. Now it was his turn to glance at Chris, for they both knew Hobie's lapses weren't caused by a yearning to catch. They happened when his attention turned more to helping Chris than to playing his own position.

Next day's practice started with Chris at first. Pete Roberts moved to left field, and Bill Ryder joined the baserunners. Chris decided he needn't feel too sorry for Bill. He was only eleven, and would have another chance next year.

Chris had thought the Millbrook style of play was about as serious as Little League baseball could get. But now he found that, compared to preparation for the tournament, the season's play had been strictly kid stuff. The all-stars practiced for hours every day. In the intervals of rest from throwing, batting or fielding practice, Mr. Snedecker lectured on signals and strategy.

The day of the first game, against the near-by small town of Galen, there was no practice. Chris stayed home, helping his mother with household chores, reading, listening to the radio—anything to keep from thinking about the game. It seemed strange that Hobie didn't drop in or phone. But Chris supposed he, too, must be resting up for the game.

The boys were to go by bus to the neutral field where the game would be played. When it was time to leave, Hobie wasn't there. Everyone got on board. The driver started the engine. Still, no Hobie.

At last Mr. Snedecker explained. "Hobie can't be here. He's sick. Nothing serious—just some virus that's going around. The doctor says he'll be fine in a day or two."

Chris's heart sank. What would he do without

Hobie to help him keep his magic working? When they took the field for practice, he found it wasn't just Hobie's moral support he needed. Hobie's replacement, Bill Ryder, had been a good second baseman during the season. But after Hobie's bold, dashing speed he reminded Chris of a tortoise trying to substitute for a hare.

Millbrook lost the toss and was first up. With dismay, Chris learned that he was fourth in the order—cleanup hitter in the first tournament game.

But the final blow came just before the game, when the teams lined up along the base lines. Into the waiting silence, before the national anthem, broke a shrill, penetrating voice. "Expect anybody to believe that kid's only twelve? Fifteen's more like it—just what it says on his back. Why, he's a regular giant."

Chris felt his face redden. Before all the strange eyes, he seemed to swell to a hulking monster, heavy and stiff and more helpless than he had ever been.

His first time at the plate, Chris drew a walk from a pitcher apparently overawed by his size. The other three times he ignominiously struck out. And at first base, where as a rule he did a creditable job, he managed to make only one error simply because during the whole game he had only one chance for a putout.

But the rest of the team looked fine. Plump Johnny Kessler of the Tigers, who had struck Chris out four times in one game, allowed Galen six hits but only one run. Millbrook, with the same number of hits, racked up six runs. Charley Dawson drove in four with a bases-loaded home run. When the Millbrook *Journal* came out next day, there was a picture of Johnny and Charley right on the front page.

"So far, so good!" Mr. Snedecker said at next day's practice. "You've had your warm-up, with a team everybody knew wasn't in your class. Saturday you'll have a real game; we play Bridgeton. State champs three years out of the past five. Twice in the finals at Williamsport, and two years ago world champions. Beat Bridgeton, and there's no telling how far we'll go."

Chris, still shaken by his miserable performance in the Galen game, wondered if Mr. Snedecker would keep him in the lineup. But Hobie, still pale from his bout with virus but cocky as ever, said sternly, "Maybe you'd better stuff cotton in your ears, stupid! Why don't you do what I told you? If you did, you'd think anybody that sounded off about people being too big was talking about some other kid."

So Chris tried again, and once more the magic began to work. He felt light and limber, and everything worked out just right. He even managed, for the first time in his life, to lay down a good bunt.

CHAPTER 21

How Big Is a Giant?

THE DAY OF THE BRIDGETON GAME was clear and hot. The crowd was immense. Mostly, it was Bridgeton fans, used to seeing their teams win and looking forward to a long tournament.

Again, Millbrook lost the toss. Chris found, with mingled relief and regret, that he had been moved down the order to eighth.

Hobie led off. Jeers at his smallness, and mocking laughter from Bridgeton fans, seemed to inspire rather than disturb him. Grinning, he drove the first pitch down the middle for a single. He stole second and third, as Kayo and Pete struck out and Mark walked. But then Jerry's long fly was caught at the fence, and the inning ended scoreless.

Kayo started shakily for Millbrook, giving up

singles to the first two Bridgeton hitters and a walk to the third. Then he settled down to retire the next three in order.

Catcher Tom Scofield led off the second. Swinging too late at a fast ball, he struck out. Charley Dawson, too, was a strikeout victim, fooled by a sharply breaking curve.

As Chris stepped to the plate, he knew he couldn't expect any breaks today. After the Galen game, no pitcher would fear him. Mr. Snedecker must be sorry he'd thrown away the threat of his apparent power by putting him in the lineup. But, Chris realized suddenly, his poor showing had done the best thing possible for him. It had cut him down to the size of everybody else. He needn't worry about living up to anybody's expectations. Now he was on his own.

He looked quickly at Hobie. Hobie grinned, holding up a hand with finger and thumb close together as if saying silently, "Think small!"

Chris struck out, holding off on a three-and-two pitch that looked high and dropped just right. But this time striking out didn't make him feel stupid. He'd just been fooled by an extra-good pitcher.

The scoreless deadlock was broken in the third, when Bridgeton loaded the bases on a single followed by two walks. This time Kayo wasn't able to pitch himself out of trouble as he had in the first. The next batter laid down a bunt, and was safe when Bob tried unsuccessfully for the out at the plate. With bases still loaded, nobody out, and a run in, Kayo seemed ready to give up.

Mr. Snedecker tried to look confident as he sent Kayo to center field, and brought Charley to the mound. But to Chris the move seemed an admission of defeat. Kayo was by far Millbrook's best pitcher. Johnny Kessler was second-best, but ineligible since he'd pitched against Galen. Charley was rated a dangerous hitter but only a fair pitcher. He had a pretty good fast ball, but not much else.

But one other thing that Charley possessed was a fierce determination. When another bunt trickled toward the mound, Charley dashed in for a running pickup. He didn't settle for the sure out at first. He didn't even risk a throw. He kept going full tilt and tagged out the runner an instant before he reached the plate.

Then came a vicious grounder up the middle. Charley grabbed it and threw to Tom for the out at the plate.

Once more a Bridgeton bat connected solidly with Charley's pitch. It was a line drive toward right, that must surely score at least two runs. Hobie made a desperate stab to intercept it. He lost his footing and hit the ground hard but came up with the ball still in his glove. The inning was over, with only one run scored.

"Now, let's get it back—and a few more!" Hobie urged, as he prepared to follow Bob Foster to the plate.

Things looked promising as Bob hit a long drive toward left. But the Bridgeton fielder was there to grab it. Then, once more, Hobie sent a sizzling drive through the tight Bridgeton infield. Hobie's second hit was also Millbrook's second. But it was wasted as Kayo and Pete struck out.

Bridgeton scored again in the bottom of the fourth, so that Chris led off in the fifth with Millbrook trailing by two. And, looking toward the dugout, he saw Mr. Snedecker pulling at the bill of his cap. It was the signal for a bunt.

For a moment Chris wondered if Mr. Snedecker had suddenly lost his mind. A bunt, with nobody on base? And from a player who'd never hit anything but home runs? But—the Bridgeton outfielders were against the fence, the infielders playing back. Chris planted his feet solidly apart and drew back his bat as if he meant to hit one a mile. Then, at the last instant, he slid his hand down the bat, dropped it deftly into place as he'd learned to do only yesterday, and sent the ball rolling lazily toward a spot halfway between first base and the pitcher's mound. He was safe by a mile.

He held first while Bob flied out to the shortstop. Hobie was the next batter. Was it possible he could collect a third hit?

It was. And Chris, off with the crack of the bat, made it all the way to third. He scored when Kayo followed with a single. Hobie scored on Pete's double to tie the score. It was still tied when the inning ended.

A long stretch to stop a hot grounder and a running catch of a hard-hit fly in foul territory were Chris's contributions to a scoreless bottom of the fifth.

"Come on, Jerry—you can do it!" Hobie screamed, as the Bears' catcher walked to the plate to lead off.

From the tense faces around him, Chris knew others shared his feeling that if they didn't break the tie now they were lost. Bridgeton had been hitting Charley's pitches hard. So far, inspired fielding and a good deal of luck had stemmed the attack. But the strength of Bridgeton's batting order was due in the bottom of the sixth. To face that power with the game riding on every pitch was a lot to expect from an inexperienced pitcher and an underdog team.

Jerry, over-anxious, swung at two bad pitches, then held off on a good one. One out. Tom was up next. Nothing ruffled Tom, and he doggedly fouled off three-and-two pitches until he won himself a walk. Charley followed. Unless he hit into a double play, everything would be up to Chris.

Hitless in his previous two appearances, Charley was surely due this time. If only he could repeat what he'd done in the Galen game! A home run now would mean a two-run margin to ease the ordeal of pitching to Bridgeton in the crucial bottom of the sixth.

Charley took a ball low, then a strike just above the knee. Then came the sharp crack of a well-hit ball, as Charley sent a grounder headed like a bullet for the hole between short and third. But the Bridgeton shortstop made a diving stop, and his throw to second forced Tom. Two out.

Afterward, Chris wondered how he'd managed not to stiffen with the helpless panic that had afflicted him so often before. With the most important game of his life hanging in the balance while the Bridgeton crowd screamed for a strikeout, the pressure should have been unbearable.

But the concentrated effort of the past days paid off when it counted. Like a beginning swimmer who suddenly feels the water supporting instead of threatening him, Chris no longer had to force himself to look to the outside. He was aware of nothing except the little white sphere coming toward him.

Chris took the first pitch—a called strike just above the knee. The next was a trifle lower, for a ball. Then another strike, low and on the inside corner. Chris took a deep breath, stepped out of the box and rubbed dust on his hands. The Bridgeton pitcher wasn't going to put anything up where he wanted it.

So Chris brought himself down to the pitch, knees dipping loose and easy and bat dropping just right to meet the ball level. He ran, top speed, for first. But the feel of the impact told him he needn't hurry, even before he heard the roar of the crowd and glanced toward the outfield to see the ball still soaring, far beyond the fence. As he followed Charley across the plate, his teammates pounded him on the back, jumping and shrieking with joy until the umpire restored order. Then Bob, almost unnoticed, struck out to end the inning.

Still, no one felt safe. Charley was still a third-string pitcher facing the best hitters of a powerful team.

The Bridgeton left fielder was a strongly-built boy, heavier than Chris though a few inches shorter. In the earlier innings he'd drawn two bases on balls, then hit a drive that Pete had grabbed with his back against the fence. Charley pitched to him too cautiously, missing the strike zone four times in a row.

Next came the wiry shortstop who'd made the incredible stop of Charley's grounder in the top of the inning. He'd been Kayo's first strikeout, but then had come up with two successive walks. If he could draw another, two men would be on base. But this time Charley managed to get his three-and-two pitch on the inside corner for the first out.

Now the batter was the Bridgeton first baseman, a left-handed hitter who'd had good wood on the ball each of his three times at bat. He'd driven in the first Bridgeton run, and later sent Kayo to the fence for a catch.

Chris looked anxiously at Charley. His shirt was soaked with sweat, but his face had a sickly pallor. His hands trembled as he picked up the rosin bag.

"Take your time, Charley," Chris called encouragingly.

Charley nodded, and bared his teeth in what was meant for a smile. He seemed near the end of his endurance. His first pitch was so low Tom had to scramble for it in the dirt, but a good pickup scared the runner back to first.

Charley's second effort was better aimed but with no steam behind it. The batter sent a sharp drive toward right field. Chris tried but knew he couldn't get it. He'd been playing near first, concentrating on holding the runner close. And it was so far over Hobie's head that nobody could expect— But, with an incredible, soaring leap Hobie pulled it in. The Bridgeton runner, halfway to second, yelped in astonishment and whirled toward first. But Hobie's throw was on its way almost before his feet had touched the ground. Chris found the bag with his foot as he took it, but to make double sure he tagged the runner hard across the letters.

There was a moment of hushed disbelief. Then the park exploded in noise and movement, as people realized it was all over. Millbrook had beaten the seemingly invincible Bridgeton. And it was Hobie who'd done it. Little Hobie, in the position he'd so nearly refused to play.

"Boy, Hobe! You did it! That was the greatest play I ever saw." Wild with delight, Chris grabbed Hobie under the arms and swung him high in the air. He felt hardly heavier than Hilda or Tina.

"You kidding?" Hobie protested. "You're the one! That ball you hit never landed—it went into orbit."

"Hold it!" a man's voice called. Chris was so startled he almost dropped Hobie. Then he saw that the man had a camera aimed at them.

"Great shot!" the man cried. "Just hold it for one more. This will make some papers outside Millbrook, or I miss my guess. And I've got the perfect caption and story":

HOW BIG IS A GIANT?
A giant Little Leaguer hit the longest home run ever. And then a midget Little Leaguer wrapped up the win with a double play nobody would believe if he hadn't seen it.

Chris set Hobie down, wishing he'd never picked him up. If this picture got spread around, calling attention to how small Hobie was, he'd probably never speak to him again.

But Hobie didn't seem worried. He stared at the

photographer, all wide-eyed, baby-faced innocence. "What's this yaketing about giants and midgets, mister? Can't you see me and my buddy are exactly the same size?"

"That's right," Chris agreed, almost exploding with laughter. "Just *precisely* the same size."

The photographer scratched his head. "Mr. Snedecker!" he said, "I think you'd better put these boys under a cold shower. The heat's got 'em. But first, how about a picture of you standing between them?"

"All right, sir!" Mr. Snedecker stepped between Chris and Hobie. When the shutter had snapped, he smiled fondly down at Hobie, then up at Chris. "But it's true, you know. They *are* the same size. Just the *right* size. Same as Johnny and Charley, the ones you were taking pictures of the other day after the Galen game. Same as whoever you'll be wanting to take pictures of a few days from now, after the Bayport game. They're all just the size it takes to do the job. Am I right, boys?"

There was no answer. Chris and Hobie were already halfway to the refreshment stand. In spite of the difference in their size, they managed to keep in perfect step as they trotted along.

"Boy, Chris!" Hobie complained. "Imagine Mr.

Snedecker wanting us to stand around while those guys hog all the free soda!"

"Pretty bad," Chris agreed. "Who wants to waste time talking about a ball game when it's over? Let's see if the rest of the fellows want to go for a swim."